COAST TO COAST, THE CRITICS HAIL QB VII

"Fast, exciting tale . . . A smashing trial scene, probably the best thing Uris has ever written."
—CLEVELAND PLAIN DEALER

"The trial is staged deliberately, dramatically . . . Uris has captured with surprising fidelity the dignity, propriety and formal manners of the British superior courts. Once Uris gets you into the courtroom, he'll have you hanging on every word."
—SATURDAY REVIEW SYNDICATE

"Entertainment, intrigue and information . . . An absorbing book."
—PITTSBURGH PRESS

"Leon Uris has written a dramatic and emotionally charged story . . . Intriguing to the last sentence of the last page."
—HOUSTON CHRONICLE

"This is a very exciting yarn, with good suspense, awesome characterizations, a provocative message and some of the best courtroom narrative you'll read anywhere."
—PHILADELPHIA BULLETIN

"A spellbinding storyteller . . . It is a pleasure to read Uris at his angry best."
—ST. LOUIS POST-DISPATCH

"Leon Uris has the great gift of writing in such a way that he reaches out and touches readers, and the touch transfers instant communication. In summary, [QB VII is] Leon Uris at his best."
—DALLAS TIMES HERALD

Bantam Books by Leon Uris
Ask your bookseller for the books you have missed

ABC-TV
SCREEN GEMS PRESENTS
THE DOUGLAS S. CRAMER PRODUCTION

QB VII

Starring
BEN GAZZARA

Co-Starring
ANTHONY HOPKINS
LESLIE CARON

Special Guest Stars in Order of Appearance
JULIET MILLS
DAN O'HERLIHY
ROBERT STEPHENS
ANTHONY QUAYLE
MILO O'SHEA
JOHN GIELGUD
DAME EDITH EVANS
JACK HAWKINS

and

LEE REMICK
as
Lady Margaret

Written for television by:
EDWARD ANHALT
Produced by: DOUGLAS S. CRAMER
Directed by: TOM GRIES

I dedicate this book
to my darling wife
JILL
On her twenty-third birthday
And to
Charlie Goldberg

ASPEN, COLORADO
APRIL 16, 1970

AUTHOR'S NOTE

THE ENGLISH LEGAL PROFESSION ADHERES TO AN
EXTREMELY FORMAL PROTOCOL AND A RIGID ETI-
QUETTE. I HAVE NOT ATTEMPTED TO BIND MYSELF
TO ALL THESE CUSTOMS BUT HAVE USED A REASON-
ABLE LITERARY LICENSE SO LONG AS THE NOVEL
REMAINS WITHIN A FRAMEWORK OF BASIC TRUTH
AND CREDIBILITY.

THE CHARACTERS CONTAINED HEREIN ARE PURELY
FICTITIOUS.

LEON URIS

QB VII

Leon Uris

BANTAM BOOKS
TORONTO · NEW YORK · LONDON

RL 8, IL 9+

QB VII

*A Bantam Book / published by arrangement with
Doubleday & Company, Inc.*

PRINTING HISTORY

Doubleday edition published November 1970

2nd printing .. November 1970	6th printing .... April 1971
3rd printing .. November 1970	7th printing .... July 1971
4th printing .. December 1970	8th printing .... August 1971
5th printing .... March 1971	9th printing ...... October 1971

Literary Guild edition published January 1971

*Bantam edition / January 1972
21 printings through November 1979*

ISBN 0–553–13702–6

Published simultaneously in the United States and Canada

---

*Bantam Books are published by Bantam Books, Inc. Its trade-
mark, consisting of the words "Bantam Books" and the por-
trayal of a bantam, is Registered in U.S. Patent and Trademark
Office and in other countries. Marca Registrada. Bantam
Books, Inc., 666 Fifth Avenue, New York, New York 10019.*

PRINTED IN THE UNITED STATES OF AMERICA

i/the plaintiff

November 1945—Monza, Italy

The corporal cadet stepped out of the guard hut and squinted out over the field. A shadowy figure ran through the knee-high grass toward him. The guard lifted a pair of binoculars. The man, half stumbling, carried a single battered suitcase. He waved and gasped a greeting in Polish.

It was a familiar sight these days. In the backwash of the war, all of Europe had become a tangled river of refugees, east going west, west going east, and burgeoning refugee camps all but collapsed under the swell. Hundreds of thousands of liberated Polish slaves roamed about desperately seeking contact with their countrymen. Many wound up here in Monza at the Fifteenth Free Polish Fighter Wing of the Royal Air Force.

"Hello! Hello!" the man shouted as he crossed out of the field and over a dusty road. His run had slowed to a limp.

The corporal cadet stepped up to him. The man was tall and slender with a high-boned face capped with a head of solid white hair.

"Polish, Free Polish?"

"Yes," the guard answered, "let me take your suitcase."

The man leaned against the guard to stave off fainting.

"Easy, father, easy. Come, sit down inside my hut. I will call for an ambulance."

The guard took him by the arm and led him. The man stopped suddenly and stared at the flag of Poland which flew from its staff just inside the gate and tears came to his eyes. He sat on a wooden bench and held his face in his hands.

The corporal cadet set the suitcase down and circled the handle of the field phone. "Post number four, send an ambulance. Yes, a refugee."

As the man was driven into the confines of the camp, the guard shook his head. Ten a day? A hundred some days. What could be done but put a few hot meals into their shrunken bellies, scrub them, give them shots against the raging diseases, a set of ragged clothing, and then dispatch them to a refugee center girding for a terrible winter. Europe would be one large house of death when the snows came.

The bulletin board in the officer's club carried a daily list of refugee arrivals. These Free Polish sought the miracle of contact with a relative or even an old friend. On some rare occasions there would be an emotional reunion of old schoolmates. Almost never was there a meeting of loved ones.

Major Zenon Myslenski entered the club, still dressed in flight jacket and fur-lined boots. He was warmly greeted, for Myslenski, with twenty-two kills of German aircraft, was one of the few quadruple aces of the Free Poles and a legend in a time of legends. He stopped automatically at the bulletin board and glanced at the new orders, the list of social events. There was a chess tournament he must enter. He was about to turn away when he was drawn to that frustrating catalogue, the new refugee list. Only four arrivals today. It was so futile.

"Hey, Zenon," someone called from the bar. "You're late."

Major Myslenski froze, eyes fixed on a name on the refugee list. Arrived, November 5—Adam Kelno.

Zenon knocked once, then burst the door open. Adam Kelno was half asleep on the cot. At first Zenon did not recognize his cousin. God, he had aged. At the outbreak of the war he didn't have a gray hair in his head. He was so bony and drawn. Through a haze, Adam Kelno felt the presence of someone. He groggily propped on an elbow and blinked his eyes.

"Zenon?"

"Cousin—"

Colonel C. Gajnow, Commander of the Fifteenth Fighter Wing, poured himself a stiff shot of vodka and lifted the pages of a preliminary interrogation of Dr. Adam Kelno, who had petitioned to be allowed to join the Free Polish Forces.

ADAM KELNO, M.D.—Born near the village of Pzetzeba, 1905. Educated—University of Warsaw, Medical College. Entered practice as a physician/surgeon in 1934.

There was testimony by his cousin, Major Zenon Myslenski, that Kelno was always identified with Polish Nationalist movements even as a student. At the beginning of World War II, with Poland occupied by the Germans, Kelno and his wife, Stella, immediately went into the Nationalist underground.

After several months their activities were discovered by the Gestapo. Stella Kelno was shot to death by a firing squad.

By a miracle Adam Kelno was spared and sent to the infamous Jadwiga Concentration Camp located midway between Krakow and Tornow in the southern region of Poland. It was an enormous manufacturing complex to feed the German war machine and manned by hundreds of thousands of slaves.

The report continued on that Kelno became a leading figure among the prisoner/doctors and did much to lift the primitive medical facilities. Kelno personally was a selfless and dedicated physician.

Later in the war when extermination facilities were introduced into Jadwiga, Kelno was responsible for saving thousands of lives from the gas chambers by falsifying reports and death certificates, through the underground and by his medical skill.

He became so prominent that toward the end of the war, the chief German medical officer, SS Dr. Colonel Adolph Voss, took Kelno, against his will, to help him run an exclusive private clinic in East Prussia.

At the end of the war, Kelno returned to Warsaw, where he ran into a shattering experience. The Polish Communists had betrayed that country to the Soviet Union. During his stay in Jadwiga, as a member of the Nationalist underground, he was constantly in a life and death struggle with the Communist underground. Now, many Communist doctors, most of them Jews, had rigged a conspiracy against Kelno with statements that he had collaborated with the Nazis. With a warrant out for his arrest, Adam Kelno fled immediately and made his way across Europe to Italy, where he made contact with the Free Polish.

Colonel Gajnow set the report down and called for his secretary. "On the Kelno matter," he said, "I am declaring a commission of inquiry to be composed of five officers with myself as chairman. We shall inquire immediately to all Free Polish Forces and organizations which may have knowledge of Kelno and we shall convene for consideration in three months."

When Poland fell in World War II and was divided between Germany and the Soviet Union by pact, many thousands of soldiers were able to escape. A government-in-exile was formed in London and fighting units put into the field and in the skies under British command.

During the war many thousands of other Polish officers fled to the Soviet Union, where they were interned and later massacred in the Katyn Forest. The Soviets had designs to take over Poland and naturally a Nationalist officer corps stood as a threat to this ambition. At the end of the war, the Soviet Army stood at the gates of Warsaw and did not budge to assist the Nationalist underground in an uprising but allowed the Germans to destroy them.

The Free Poles were to remain in England, rightfully bitter, tightly knit, and forever fanning the dream of a return to their homeland. When the call went out on the matter of Adam Kelno it quickly reached the entire Polish Community.

On the face of it, things seemed clear enough. Dr. Adam Kelno was a Polish Nationalist and when he returned to Warsaw he was to be eliminated by the Communists just as the officer corps had been in the Katyn Massacre.

Within days of the launching of the inquiry, sworn statements began to come back to Monza along with offers of personal testimony.

I HAVE KNOWN DR. ADAM KELNO FROM 1942, WHEN I WAS SENT TO JADWIGA CONCENTRATION CAMP. I BECAME ILL AND TOO WEAK TO WORK. HE HID ME AND SAVED ME FROM THE GERMANS. HE SAVED MY LIFE.

DR. ADAM KELNO OPERATED ON ME AND NURSED ME
BACK TO HEALTH WITH GREAT CARE.

DR. KELNO HELPED ARRANGE MY ESCAPE FROM JADWIGA.

DR. KELNO OPERATED ON ME AT FOUR O'CLOCK IN THE
MORNING WHEN HE WAS SO TIRED HE COULD HARDLY
STAND UP. I DON'T THINK HE EVER SLEPT FOR MORE
THAN A FEW HOURS AT A TIME.

HE SAVED MY LIFE.

On the day of the commission, the camp was visited by
Leopold Zalinski, a legendary figure of the Polish Nationalist
underground during the occupation. His code name, Kon,
was known by every Pole. Kon's testimony erased any
doubts. He swore Adam Kelno to be a hero of the Nationalist underground before his imprisonment and during his
years as a prisoner/doctor at Jadwiga. With letters and testi-
monies from two dozen others without conflict, the commission cleared him.

In a moving ceremony at Monza attended by many Polish
colonels of the Free Forces, Dr. Adam Kelno was sworn in
as a captain and his pips were pinned on him by his cousin.

Poland had been taken from these men but they continued
to remember and dream.

2

The Sixth Polish Hospital-
Foxfield Cross Camp-
Tunbridge Wells, England—March 1946

Major Adam Kelno walked slowly from the surgery tugging
at his rubber gloves. Sister Angela untied his surgical mask
and dabbed the perspiration from his head.

"Where is she?" Adam asked.

"In the visitor's lounge. Adam?"

"Yes."

"Will you come to my flat?"

"Yes, all right."

"I'll wait."

As he walked the long dim corridor, it was obvious Angela Brown's admiration was more than professional. It had been but a few short months that they had worked together in surgery. From the onset she was impressed by his skill and a kind of dedicated zeal in which he performed half as many operations again as most of his colleagues. His hands were magnificent.

It all happened rather plainly. Angela Brown, a commonplace sort in her mid-thirties, had been a capable nurse for a decade. A first short marriage ended in divorce. The great love of her life, a Polish flyer in the RAF, was shot down over the Channel.

Adam Kelno was nothing like her fighter pilot so it became a new kind of love. A rather magic spot in time the instant he peered over his mask and caught her eye as she placed instruments in his hands, his quick decisive hands and the closeness of spirit as they worked together as a team to save a human life. The exhilaration of a successful operation. The exhaustion of a failure after a difficult battle.

They were so lonely, both of them, and so it happened in a very undramatic but lovely manner.

Adam entered the visitor's lounge. It was very late. The operation had lasted more than three hours. There was a look of stunned anticipation on Madame Baczewski's face. Afraid to ask. Adam took her hand, bowed slightly and kissed it, then sat beside her.

"Jerzy has left us. It was very peaceful."

She nodded, but dared not speak.

"Is there anyone I should call, Madame Baczewski?"

"No. There was only us. We are the only survivors."

"I think we had better put you in a room here."

She tried to speak but her mouth went into a trembling spasm and tiny little grunts of agony emerged. "He said

. . . get me to Dr. Kelno . . . he kept me alive in the concentration camp . . . get me to Dr. Kelno."

Angela arrived and took charge. Adam whispered to have her put under.

"When I first met Jerzy Baczewski he was so strong like a bull. He was a great Pole, one of our foremost dramatists. We knew the Germans were out to destroy the intelligentsia and we had to keep him alive at any price. This surgery was not that difficult. A healthy man would have gotten through this, but he had no stamina left after two years in that putrid hell hole."

"Darling, it was you that told me a good surgeon has to be impersonal. You did everything. . . ."

"Sometimes I don't believe my own words. Jerzy died a betrayed man. Lonely, his country taken from him, and a memory of unbelievable terror."

"Adam, you've been in surgery half the night. Here, darling, take your tea."

"I want a drink."

He poured a stiff one, tossed it down, and poured another. "All Jerzy wanted was a child. What kind of a damned tragedy are we? What kind of curse is on us? Why can't we live?"

The bottle was empty. He chewed at his knuckles.

Angela ran her fingers through that thicket of white hair. "Will you stay tonight?"

"I would like that. I don't want to be alone."

She sat on the footstool before him and lay her head in his lap. "Dr. Novak called me aside today," she said. "He told me to get you out of the hospital for a little rest or you're going to break down."

"What the hell does August Novak know. A man who has spent his life fixing oversized noses and transplanting hair for balding British gentry in his singular quest for knighthood. Get me another drink."

"My God, turn it off."

As he began to arise she grabbed his hands and held him, then looked pleading and kissed his fingers, each one.

"Don't cry, Angela, please don't cry."

"My auntie has a lovely little cottage at Folkestone. We're welcome there if we want to go."

"Perhaps I am a little tired," he said.

The days at Folkestone all went so quickly. He was renewed by long quiet walks along the leas on the cliffs overlooking the sea. France was across the Channel in shadowy outline. Hand in hand in silent communication they walked wind-blown along the shrub-lined rosemary path to the harbor and in the distance the sounds of the band concert at the Marine Gardens. The narrow little streets had been bombed out but the statue of William Harvey, the discoverer of the circulation of the blood, remained. The steamer to Calais left daily again and soon there would be vacationers for the short summer season.

The evening chill was dulled by a crackling fire that threw odd shadows over the old low-beamed ceiling of the cottage. The last lovely day had ended and tomorrow they would return to the hospital.

A sudden moroseness came over Adam. He drank rather heavily. "I'm sorry it's over," he mumbled. "I don't remember such a beautiful week."

"It need not end," she said.

"Everything for me must end. I can have nothing that is not taken from me. Everyone I have ever loved has been taken from me. My wife, my mother, my brothers. Any who have survived are in virtual slavery in Poland. I can make no commitments, never again."

"I've never asked for one," she said.

"Angela, I want to love you, but you see, if I do, I'll lose you too."

"What's the difference, Adam. We'll end up losing each other without even giving it a chance."

"There's more to it, you know that. I am afraid for myself as a man. I have this deadly fear of impotence and it's not the drinking that does it. It's . . . so many things that happened in that place."

"I'll keep you strong, Adam," she said.

He reached out and touched her cheek and she kissed his hands. "Your hands. Your beautiful hands."

"Angela, would you give me a child right away?"

"Yes, my darling darling."

Angela became pregnant a few months after their marriage.

Dr. August Novak, executive surgeon of the Sixth Polish Hospital, returned to private practice and in a surprise move, Adam Kelno was moved over a number of seniors to be named head of the hospital.

Administrative work was not what Adam desired but the enormous responsibilities at the Jadwiga Concentration Camp had trained him for it. Along with budgets and politics, he managed to keep his sure hand in as a surgeon.

It was so good to come home these days. The Kelno cottage in Groombridge Village was a few miles from the hospital at Tunbridge Wells. Angela's belly was filling beautifully with their child and in the evenings they would walk, as always, hand in hand in communicative silence up the wooded path to Toad Rock and take their tea at the quaint little café. Adam drank much less these days.

On an evening in July he signed out at the hospital and his orderly put the groceries in the rear seat of his car. He drove to the center of town and in the Pantiles Colonnade he bought a bouquet of roses and made for Groombridge.

Angela did not answer to his ring. This always gave him a start. The fear of losing her hovered behind every tree of the forest. Adam juggled the grocery sack and fished for his key. Wait! The door was not locked. He opened it.

"Angela!"

His wife sat on the edge of a chair in the living room, ashen-faced. Adam's eyes went to the two men hovering over her.

"Dr. Kelno?"

"Yes."

"Inspector Ewbank, Scotland Yard."

"Inspector Henderson," the second man said, holding out his identification.

"What do you want? What are you doing here?"

"I have a warrant for your arrest, sir."

"My arrest?"

"Yes, sir."

"What is this all about? What kind of joke is this?"

Their sullen expressions denoted it was no joke.

"My arrest . . . for what?"

"You are to be detained at Brixton Prison pending extradition to Poland to stand charges as a war criminal."

3

The setting was London but the room seemed something out of Warsaw. Angela sat in the anteroom of the Society of Free Poles where walls were adorned with enormous sterile paintings of Pilsudski, Smigly-Rydz, Paderewski, and a gallery of Polish heroes. It was in this place and others like it around London that the hundred thousand Poles fortunate enough to escape perpetuated the dream of Poland.

Angela's pregnancy now showed heavily. Zenon Myslenski comforted her as she wrung and knotted a handkerchief nervously. A tall door opened from an inner office and a secretary approached them.

Angela adjusted her dress and waddled in on Zenon's arm where Count Anatol Czerny came from behind his desk. He greeted Zenon as an old friend, kissed Angela's hand, and bade them be seated.

"I am afraid," the dapper little aristocrat said, "valuable time has been wasted by contacting the government-in-exile. England no longer recognizes them, and we were unable to get any information from the British Home Office."

"What in the name of God is it all about? Someone has to tell us something," Angela emoted.

"All we know is that about a fortnight ago a certain

Nathan Goldmark arrived from Warsaw. He is a Jewish Communist and a special investigator for the Polish Secret Police. He has a number of sworn statements from ex-inmates of Jadwiga, all Polish Communists, making various allegations against your husband."

"What kind of allegations?"

"I have not seen them and the Home Office is most secretive. The British position is this. If a foreign government with whom they have a mutual pact requests extradition and establishes a prima facie case, they treat the matter as routine."

"But what possible charges could there be against Adam. You've read the testimony from the investigation in Monza. I was there myself," Zenon said.

"Well, we both really know what is happening, don't we," the count answered.

"No, I don't understand it at all," Angela said.

"The Communists feel it necessary to keep up a constant parade of propaganda to justify their seizure of Poland. Dr. Kelno is intended as a sacrificial lamb. What better way than to prove a Nationalist was a war criminal."

"What in the name of God can we do?"

"We will fight this thing, of course. We are not without recourses. It will take a few weeks for the Home Office to review the matter. Our first tactic is to get a delay. Madame Kelno, I want the liberty of engaging a firm of solicitors who have been most helpful to us in these matters."

"Yes, of course," she whispered.

"Hobbins, Newton, and Smiddy."

"Oh, my poor darling Adam. . . . Oh, dear God."

"Angela, please."

"Are you all right, Madame Kelno?"

"Yes. . . . I'm sorry." She pressed her white folded knuckles to her lips and drew deep sighs.

"Come now," Count Czerny said. "We are in England. We are dealing with a decent, civilized people."

The Austin taxi stopped in the center of the Pall Mall, found an opening in the opposite flow of traffic, and did a swift U-turn in a circle no larger than a halfpenny, stopping before the Reform Club.

Richard Smiddy jammed his bowler on tightly, tucked his umbrella under an arm, opened a tattered change purse and carefully doled out the exact fare.

"And a sixpence for you," he said.

"Thank you, governor," the cabbie said, putting on his FOR HIRE light and pulling away from the curb. He shook his head as he pocketed the frail tip. Not that he wanted the war, mind you, but he wished the Yanks were back.

Richard Smiddy, son of George Smiddy and grandson of Harold Smiddy of that fine old law firm marched the stairs to the entrance of the Reform Club. He was rather pleased about getting an appointment with Robert Highsmith in less than a week. As protocol required, Smiddy's clerk wrote a hand-delivered note to Highsmith's clerk at Parliament and arranged the meeting. Smiddy did have his man denote that the matter had some urgency. For a passing moment Richard Smiddy had contemplated by-passing tradition and picking up the telephone but only the Americans did business that way.

He deposited his umbrella and bowler with the hall porter and made the usual remark about the foul weather.

"Mr. Highsmith is expecting you, sir."

Smiddy trotted up the stairs to that place where Phileas Fogg began and ended his trip around the world in eighty days, then into the lounge off to the right. Robert Highsmith, a heavily set fellow indifferently tailored, moved his largeness from a deep leather chair that was cracked with age. Highsmith was somewhat of a colorful character having bolted a family of landed gentry to be called to the bar. He was a dazzling barrister of extraordinary skill and, at the age of thirty-five, recently elected to the House of Commons. A zealous crusader by nature, Highsmith always seemed to have his finger in some pudding of injustice. As such he headed the British office of Sanctuary International, an organization devoted to the defense of political prisoners.

"Hello there, Smiddy, sit down, sit down."

"Good of you to see me so soon."

"Not soon enough. I had to put a lot of pressure on the

Home Office to hold things off. You should have phoned me for an appointment with time so short."

"Well yes, that did occur to me."

Highsmith ordered a whisky neat and Richard Smiddy ordered tea and cakes.

"Well, I've got the gist of the charges," Highsmith said. "They want him for just about everything in the book." He balanced his specs on the end of his nose, brushed back his disheveled hair, and read from a single sheet of paper. "Giving fatal shots of phenol to prisoners, collaboration with the Nazis, selecting prisoners for the gas chambers, participating in experimental surgery, taking an oath as an honorary German. And so forth, and so forth. Sounds like a bloody monster. What kind of a chap is he?"

"Decent enough sort. A bit blunt. Polish, you know."

"What's your office got to say about all this?"

"We've gone over the matter very carefully, Mr. Highsmith, and I'd wager my last quid that he's innocent."

"Bastards. Well, we're not going to let them get away with it."

Sanctuary International
Raymond Buildings
Gray's Inn
London WC 1

The Under Secretary of State
Home Office
Aliens Department
10 Old Bailey
London EC 4

Dear Mr. Clayton-Hill,

I had advised you earlier of the interest of Sanctuary International in the matter of Dr. Adam Kelno, now being detained in H.M. Prison at Brixton. As a matter of procedure, our organization looks with suspicion on any demands for political prisoners being extradited to Communist states. Dr. Kelno is clearly a political victim.

On further scrutiny it is our belief that the charges against Dr. Kelno appear to be totally without foundation. The affidavits against him are either from Polish Communists or Communist-oriented persons.

In no event has anyone claimed to have personally witnessed any wrong doing by Dr. Kelno. These affidavits are based on the loosest kind of hearsay that would be inadmissible evidence in any court of law in the Western world. Furthermore, the Polish government has been unable to produce a single victim of Dr. Kelno's alleged cruelty.

In our opinion Poland has absolutely failed to establish a prima facie case. Those persons who are able to testify to Dr. Kelno's magnificent behavior in Jadwiga cannot go to Poland and under no circumstances will the man be given a fair trial. If this extradition is permitted it would be tantamount to a political murder.

In the name of British fair play, Sanctuary International pleads for the unconditional release of this blameless man.

Yours faithfully,

Robert Highsmith

> Hobbins, Newton & Smiddy
> Solicitors
> 32B Chancery Lane
> London WC 2

The Under Secretary of State
Home Office
Aliens Department
10 Old Bailey
London EC 4

Re: Dr. Adam Kelno

Dear Mr. Clayton-Hill,

Further to the matter of Dr. Adam Kelno. I have the pleasure of enclosing twenty more statements from former inmates of the Jadwiga Concentration Camp on behalf of our client.

We are appreciative of your granting a delay which has allowed us to bring forth over a hundred affidavits. However, Dr. Kelno has been in prison for nearly six months without a prima facie case against him.

We shall be obliged if you will inform us whether you are now satisfied on the evidence we have produced and can arrange to release Dr. Kelno or if we are to go to further expense and labor.

May I call your attention to an honorary tribunal consisting of representatives of all the Free Polish organizations which has not only exonerated him but cites him as a hero.

Faithfully yours,

Hobbins, Newton & Smiddy

In the House of Commons, Robert Highsmith gained support from his fellow members and exerted growing pressure for the release of Kelno. A rash of opinion was growing against the obvious injustice.

Yet, equally insistent was a feeling of anger from Poland that a beastly war criminal was at large and being protected by the British. From their point of view it was a Polish matter and England was bound by treaty to return him for trial.

Just as it seemed that Sanctuary International was turning the corner, Nathan Goldmark, the Polish investigator who was in England pressing for the extradition, found an unexpected witness.

4

The skyline of Oxford was punctured by a hundred spires and towers. Nathan Goldmark of the Polish Secret Police nibbled on his knuckles and pressed close to the train window as fellow passengers pulled their luggage down from the overhead rack.

Oxford, he had read on the ride up from London, dated back to the twelfth century and had grown to its present conglomerate of thirty-one colleges with assorted cathedrals, hospitals, institutions, all joggled about in winding ways, a terribly romantic stream, Gothic richness, fluted ceilings, ancient quadrangles, and the chancellors, and masters, and readers, and students, and choirs. Colleges such as the Magdalenes and Pembrokes and All Souls counted their history and their heroes in hundreds of years. The Nuffields and St. Catherine's in mere decades. All of it was filled with the roll call of immortals that was the greatness of England itself.

Nathan Goldmark found the taxi stand and handed the driver a slip of paper that read, Radcliffe Medical Center. He lowered his window despite the chill drizzle as they drove toward a flood of bicycles and jaunty students. On an ancient wall in paint in red letters were the words, JESUS WAS A FAIRY.

In the sterile sanctuary of the medical center he was taken down a long corridor, past a dozen laboratories to the tiny, disheveled office of Dr. Mark Tesslar, who had been expecting him.

"We will go to my place," Tesslar said. "It is better to speak there."

Tesslar's apartment was a few miles from the center of Oxford in the countryside, in a converted monastery at Wytham Abbey. It took only a moment or so for Dr. Mark Tesslar and Nathan Goldmark to size each other up, for they were both members of the same unique club, the few and far between Polish Jews to survive Hitler's holocaust. Tesslar had matriculated through the Warsaw Ghetto, Majdanek and Jadwiga Concentration Camps. Goldmark was a graduate of Dachau and Auschwitz. The rivulets of deep furrows and sunken eyes betrayed the past of one to the other.

"How did you find me, Goldmark?" Tesslar asked.

"Through Dr. Maria Viskova. She told me you were in Oxford working on special research."

The mention of Maria brought a smile to an otherwise rigid, bony face. "Maria . . . when did you see her last?"

"A week ago."

"How is she?"

"Well, in a favorable position but, like all of us, trying to find out where life is again. Trying to understand what happened."

"I begged her, when we were liberated and returned to Warsaw, to leave Poland. It is no place for a Jew. It's a graveyard. A vast, hollow place filled with the smell of death."

"But you are still a Polish citizen, Dr. Tesslar."

"No. I have no intentions of going back. Never."

"It will be a great loss for the Jewish community."

"What Jewish community? A smattering of ghosts sifting through the ashes."

"It will be different now."

"Will it, Goldmark? Then why do they have a separate branch of the Communist Party for Jews. I'll tell you. Because the Poles won't admit to their guilt and they have to keep what is left of the Jews locked in Poland. See! We have Jews here. They like it here. We are good Poles. And people like you do their dirty work. You have to keep a Jewish community in Poland to justify your own existence. You're being used. But in the end you'll find out the Communists are no better for us than the Nationalists before the war. Inside that country we are pigs."

"And Maria Viskova . . . a lifelong Communist?"

"She will be disenchanted too, before it's over."

Goldmark wished to disengage the conversation. His face pinched nervously as he sucked at one cigarette after the other. As Tesslar made his attack, Goldmark became more restless.

Mark Tesslar limped slightly as he took the tray of tea from his housekeeper. He prepared it and poured.

"The reason of my visit to Oxford," Goldmark said, "concerns Adam Kelno."

The mention of Kelno's name brought an instant visible reaction. "What about Kelno?"

Goldmark smirked a little, chomping with the sudden importance of his revelation. "You've known him a long time?"

"Since we were students in 1930."

"When was the last you saw of him?"

"Leaving the Jadwiga Concentration Camp. I heard he came to Warsaw after the war, then fled."

"What would you say if I told you he was in England?"

"Free?"

"Not exactly. He is being detained at the Brixton Prison. We are trying to get him extradited to Poland. You ought to know the situation here in England with the Polish fascists. They have made a cause célèbre out of him. They've managed to attract enough attention in high places to make the British do a fence-sitting act. You knew him intimately in Jadwiga?"

"Yes," Tesslar whispered.

"Then you must be aware of the charges against him."

"I know he committed experimental surgery on our people."

"How do you know this?"

"I saw it with my own eyes."

The Under Secretary of State
The Home Office
Alien's Department
10 Old Bailey
London EC 4

Hobbins, Newton & Smiddy
Solicitors
32B Chancery Lane
London WC 2

Re: Dr. Adam Kelno

Gentlemen:

I am directed by the Secretary of State to inform you that he has carefully considered all the circumstances including information furnished by the Polish government. With the recent sworn statement of Dr. Mark Tesslar the Secretary of State considers that a prima facie case has been established. It is not within our jurisdiction to comment on the right or wrong of Polish law but to comply with treaties in effect with that government.

Therefore, the Secretary of State has decided to enforce the deportation order by sending Dr. Kelno to Poland.

I am, gentlemen,

Your obedient servant,

John Clayton-Hill

5

The guard led Adam Kelno into the glassed consultation room where he was seated opposite Robert Highsmith and Richard Smiddy.

"I'm going to come right to the point, Kelno," Highsmith said, "we are in a nasty bind. Nathan Goldmark has obtained a very damaging affidavit against you. What does the name Mark Tesslar mean to you?"

Fear was evident in him.

"Well?"

"He is in England?"

"Yes."

"It is all very clear. Once the Polish government could

not establish a case against me, they sent one of them after me."

"One of whom?"

"The Communists. The Jews."

"What about Tesslar?"

"He swore to get me almost twenty years ago." Kelno hung his head. "Oh God, what's the use."

"See here, man, you pull yourself together. There is no time for sinking spells. We have to keep our wits."

"What do you want to know?"

"When did you first meet Tesslar?"

"Around 1930 at the university when we were students together. He was dismissed for committing abortions and he claimed I was the one who turned him in. At any rate, he concluded his medical training in Europe, Switzerland, I think."

"Did you see him when he returned to Warsaw to practice before the war?"

"No, but he was a well-known abortionist. As a Roman Catholic it was difficult for me to recommend abortions, but a few times I felt it best for the life of the patient and once a close relative was in trouble. Tesslar never knew I sent people to him. It was always done through a blind party."

"Go on."

"By some insane quirk of fate I met him again in Jadwiga. His reputation preceded him. Late in 1942 the Germans took him from the Warsaw Ghetto and removed him to Majdanek Concentration Camp outside the city of Lublin. Here he was charged by the SS doctors to keep the camp prostitutes free of disease and to perform abortions when necessary."

Smiddy, who had been writing notes quickly, looked up. "How do you know this?"

"Word of this sort spreads quickly even from one camp to another. The doctors were in a very small community and a few transfers here and there would give us all the news. Also, as a member of the Nationalist underground I had access to this kind of information. We all knew about Tesslar when he arrived in Jadwiga in 1943."

"You were the chief medical officer, so you must have had close contact with him?"

"No. It was not the case. You see, there were twenty-six barracks in the medical complex but Barracks One to Five were where the SS doctors conducted secret experiments. Tesslar lived down there. It is he who should be standing trial, not me. I warned him he would have to answer for his crimes, but he was under protection of the Germans. When the war was over, Tesslar became a Communist and joined the secret police as a medical officer in order to save himself. That is when he swore those lies against me."

"I want you to answer this very carefully, Dr. Kelno," Highsmith accentuated. "Did you ever perform any amputations of testicles and ovaries?"

Kelno shrugged. "Of course. I performed ten thousand, fifteen thousand operations. Large ones, small ones. A man's testicle or a woman's ovary can become diseased like any other part of the body. When I operated, I did it to save a patient's life. I recall cancers and tumors of the sexual glands. But you see how such things can become distorted. I never operated on a healthy man."

"Who accused you of that?"

"I know all of Tesslar's accusations. Do you want to hear them? They are stamped on my brain."

"Very well," Highsmith said. "We were able to get a short delay in order to give you time to answer Tesslar's statement. You must go about it coldly, dispassionately, and honestly and don't inject your personal animosity against him. You must answer every charge, point by point. Here, study this statement tonight with great care. We will be back tomorrow with a shorthand writer to take your answer."

"I categorically deny that I boasted to Dr. Tesslar the performing of fifteen thousand experiments in surgery without anesthetic. Too many people have testified to my good behavior to make this anything but the wildest sort of slander."

"I categorically deny I ever performed surgery on a healthy man or woman. I deny I was ever inhumane to my patients. I deny ever taking part in any experimental surgery of any sort."

"It is a pure fabrication that Dr. Tesslar ever saw me perform surgery. He was never, at any time, in any theater where I operated."

"Too many of my patients are alive and have testified in my behalf to give validity to the charge that my operations were badly performed."

"It is my sincere conviction that Dr. Tesslar made these charges to take the onus of guilt off himself. I believe he was sent to England as a part of a conspiracy to destroy all remaining traces of Polish nationalism. The fact that he has asked for asylum in England is merely a Communist trick, is not to be trusted."

As the time of decision drew close, Adam Kelno went into a deep depression. Even the visits from Angela failed to lift his spirits.

She handed him a set of photographs of their son, Stephan. Adam set them down on the table without looking. "I can't," he said.

"Adam, let me bring the child so you can see him."

"No, not in a prison."

"He's only an infant. He won't remember."

"See him . . . so I can carry the tortured remembrance of him through a mock trial in Warsaw. Is that what you are trying to tell me?"

"We are fighting just as hard as ever. Only . . . I can't see you like this. We've always drawn strength from each other. How easy do you think this has been on me? I work all day, try to raise a child by myself, come to see you. Adam . . . oh, Adam . . ."

"Don't touch me, Angela. It is becoming too painful."

The special basket of food she brought to Brixton four times a week had been inspected and passed. Adam was disinterested.

"I have been here almost two years," he mumbled, "watched over like a condemned man in solitary confinement. They watch me at meal times, at the toilet. No buttons, belts, razors. Even my pencils are taken away at night. I have nothing to do but read and pray. They're right . . .

I have wanted to commit suicide. Only the thought of living to see my son as a free man has kept me alive but now . . . even that hope is gone."

John Clayton-Hill, the Under Secretary, sat down at the table across from the Secretary of State, Sir Percy Maltwood, with that damnable deportation order between them.

Maltwood had called Thomas Bannister, King's Counsel, into the Kelno affair on behalf of the Home Office to see if his opinion differed from Highsmith's.

Thomas Bannister in his early forties was a barrister of stature equal to Highsmith's. A man of average build, prematurely grayed, and ruddy English in complexion. All that seemed extraordinarily placid leaped into exquisite and brilliant action within the walls of a courtroom.

"What will your report say, Tom?" Maltwood asked.

"It will say that there is a reasonable doubt as to either Kelno's guilt or innocence and therefore the Polish government is obliged to produce more evidence. I don't think they have established a prima facie case because what it all boils down to is Tesslar's word against Kelno's."

Bannister gracefully moved into a seat and riffled through the now heavy records. "Most of the affidavits supplied by the Polish government are based on pure hearsay. We have come to know, have we not, that Tesslar is either lying to save himself or Kelno is lying to save himself. Both of them obviously dislike each other. What happened in Jadwiga happened in total secrecy so we don't really know if we would be hanging a political victim or freeing a war criminal."

"What do you think we ought to do, Tom?"

"Continue to hold him in Brixton until one side or the other comes up with concrete evidence."

"Off the record," Maltwood said, "what is your opinion?"

Bannister looked from one to the other and smiled. "Come on, Sir Percy, you know I won't answer that."

"We are going strictly on your recommendation, Tom, not your hunches."

"I think Kelno is guilty. I'm not sure of what, but he's guilty of something," Tom Bannister said.

The Polish Embassy
47 Portland Place
London, W 1
January 15, 1949

The Secretary of State

Sir:

The Polish ambassador presents his compliments to His Majesty's Principal Secretary of State for Foreign Affairs and has the honor to inform him of the Polish government's attitude on the subject of Dr. Adam Kelno. The Polish government holds the view that:

It has established beyond doubt that Dr. Adam Kelno, now under custody in Great Britain in Brixton Prison, was a surgeon in Jadwiga Concentration Camp and is suspect of having perpetrated war crimes.

Dr. Kelno is listed as a suspect war criminal by the United Nations War Crimes Commission and the governments of Czechoslovakia and the Netherlands as well as Poland.

The Polish government has supplied all required evidence to His Majesty's government sufficient for a prima facie case.

Further evidence should be preserved for the proper Polish courts.

The government of the United Kingdom must now comply with requests for the extradition of war criminals under existing treaty.

Furthermore, public opinion in Poland is outraged by this undue delay.

Therefore, for finalizing once and forever the fact that Dr. Adam Kelno should be deported to Poland, we shall produce a victim of Dr. Kelno's brutality and will, in accordance to British jurisprudence, bring forth a man who was castrated by Dr. Kelno in a brutal manner as a part of a medical experiment.

I am, sir,
Most faithfully,

Zygmont Zybowski,
Ambassador

6

Opposite glorious old Covent Garden stood that grim gray stone Palladian edifice, the Bow Street Magistrate's Court, most noted among London's fourteen police courts. A line of chauffeured limousines parked before the station testified to the importance of the occasion taking place behind the closed doors of a large, drafty, shabby conference room.

Robert Highsmith was there, hiding his tension behind a strewn posture. The proper Richard Smiddy was there, nibbling at his lower lip. The Magistrate, Mr. Griffin, was there. Nathan Goldmark, the dogged hunter, was there. John Clayton-Hill of the Home Office was there and so were officers of Scotland Yard and a shorthand writer.

Someone else was there. Thomas Bannister, K.C. Doubting Thomas, one might say.

"Shall we proceed, gentlemen," the magistrate said. Everyone nodded. "Officer. Bring in Dr. Fletcher."

Dr. Fletcher, a nondescript man, was ushered in and asked to take a seat opposite the magistrate at the end of the table. He gave his name and address to the shorthand writer. Magistrate Griffin proceeded.

"This hearing is rather informal so we shan't bind ourselves with too many rules unless counsel become argumentative. For the record, Mr. Goldmark and Mr. Clayton-Hill may ask questions. Now, Dr. Fletcher, are you a registered medical practitioner?"

"I am, sir."

"Where do you practice?"

"I am the senior medical officer at His Majesty's Prison at Wormwood Scrubbs and I am senior medical adviser to the Home Office."

"Have you examined a man named Eli Janos?"

"I have, yesterday afternoon."

The magistrate turned to the reporter. "For the sake of identification, Eli Janos is a Hungarian of Jewish ancestry now living in Denmark. At the instigation of the government of Poland, Mr. Janos volunteered to come to England. Now, Dr. Fletcher, would you be so kind as to inform us as to the finding of your examination in particular regard to Mr. Janos's testicles."

"Poor devil is a eunuch," Dr. Fletcher said.

"I should like that stricken," Robert Highsmith said unfolding himself quickly. "I don't think it's proper to inject such personal observation and editorial comment as 'poor devil.'"

"He's damned well a poor devil, isn't he, Highsmith?" Bannister said.

"I should like the Learned Magistrate to inform my learned friend here . . ."

"All of this is rather unnecessary, gentlemen," the magistrate said with a sudden show of the authority of British justice. "Mr. Highsmith, Mr. Bannister, will you stop this immediately?"

"Yes, sir."

"Sorry, sir."

"Please continue, Dr. Fletcher."

"There is no trace of testicles in the scrotal sack or the inguinal canal."

"Are there scars of an operation?"

"Yes. On both sides, just a bit over the inguinal canal, which I would deem orthodox scars for the removal of testicles."

"Can you tell the Learned Magistrate," Bannister said, "if you have an opinion as to whether or not the operation on Janos's testicles was performed in a normal, skillful way?"

"Yes, it appears to be proper surgery."

"And," Highsmith snapped, "there is nothing to show abuse, bad surgery, complications, that sort of thing?"

"No . . . I would say I saw nothing to indicate that."

Highsmith, Bannister, and the magistrate asked a number of technical questions about the manner of the operation after which Dr. Fletcher was properly thanked and dismissed.

"Bring in Eli Janos," the magistrate ordered.

Eli Janos had many of the manifestations of a eunuch. He was fat. When he spoke, his high pitched voice was broken. Magistrate Griffin personally escorted Janos to his seat. There was a beat of awkward silence.

"It is quite all right if you wish to smoke, gentlemen."

There was fishing through pockets for the relief of tobacco. Pipe, cigar, and cigarette smoke bellowed out, then drifted to the high ceiling.

Magistrate Griffin glanced through Janos's statement. "Mr. Janos, I take it you speak sufficient English so you will not need an interpreter."

"I can pass."

"If there is anything you don't understand, do ask us to repeat the question. Also, I realize that this is an ordeal for you. If, at any time, you become upset, please let me know."

"I have no more tears left for myself," he answered.

"Yes, thank you. I should first like to review some of the facts in your affidavit. You are Hungarian by birth in the year of 1920. The Gestapo found you in hiding in Budapest and transported you to the Jadwiga Concentration Camp. Before the war you were a furrier and at the concentration camp you worked in a factory making German uniforms."

"Yes, that is correct."

"In the spring of 1943 you were caught smuggling and taken before an SS tribunal. They found you guilty and sentenced you to have your testicles removed. You were then removed to the medical compound and interned in a place known as Barrack III. Four days later the operation was performed in Barrack V. You were forced at gun point to undress and were prepared by prisoner/orderlies and thence castrated by a Polish prisoner/doctor whom you accuse of being Dr. Adam Kelno."

"Yes."

"Gentlemen, you may question Mr. Janos."

"Mr. Janos," Thomas Bannister said, "I should like to establish a little more background. This charge of smuggling. What was this about?"

"We were always in company with the three angels of Jadwiga, death, hunger, and disease. You have read what has been written of these places. I do not have to elaborate. Smuggling was a normal way of life . . . normal as the fog of London. We smuggled to stay alive. Although the SS runs the camp we are guarded by Kapos. Kapos are also prisoners who earn their favor with the Germans by collaboration. The Kapos can be as brutal as the SS. It was a simple matter. I did not pay off certain Kapos so they turned me in."

"I should like to know if any of the Kapos were Jewish?" Bannister asked.

"Only a few from every hundred."

"But most of the labor was Jewish?"

"Seventy-five percent Jews. Twenty percent Poles and other Slavs and the rest criminals or political prisoners."

"And you were first taken to Barrack III."

"Yes. I learned that in this barrack the Germans kept the raw material for medical experiments . . . and then I was taken to Barrack V."

"And forced to undress and shower?"

"Yes, then I was shaved by an orderly and made to sit naked in the anteroom." Janos fished for a cigarette and his story slowed and his voice varied now with the pain of memory. "They came in, the doctor with an SS colonel. Voss, Adolph Voss."

"How do you know it was Voss?" Highsmith asked.

"He told me, and he told me that as a Jew my testicles would do no good because he was going to sterilize all the Jews so I would be serving the cause of science."

"In what language did he speak to you?"

"German."

"Are you fluent in German?"

"In a concentration camp, you learn enough German."

"And you claim," Highsmith continued, "that the doctor with him was Kelno."

"Yes."

"How did you know that?"

"In Barrack III it is known and said Dr. Kelno was the head of prisoner medicine and often performed surgery for Voss in Barrack V. I heard of no other doctor's name."

"Dr. Tesslar. Did you ever hear of him?"

"At the end of my recovery a new doctor came to Barrack III. It may have been Tesslar. The name sounds familiar, but I never met him."

"Then what happened?"

"I became panicked. Three or four orderlies held me down and another gave me an injection in the spine. Soon my lower body became dead. I was strapped to a trolley and taken into the operation room."

"Who was there?"

"The SS colonel Dr. Voss and the Polish doctor and one or two assistants. Voss said he was going to time the operation and wanted the eggs removed quickly. I begged in Polish for Kelno to leave one testicle. He only shrugged and when I screamed he slapped me and then . . . he took them out."

"So," Bannister said, "you had ample time to see this man without a surgical mask."

"He wore no mask. He did not even wash his hands. For a month after, I almost died from infection."

"To be absolutely clear," Bannister said, "you were a normal healthy man when you were taken to Barrack V."

"Weak from the concentration camp life but normal sexually."

"You had no prior treatment of X ray or anything else that could have damaged your testicles?"

"No. They only wanted to see how fast it could be done."

"And would you describe your treatment on the operating table as less than gentle."

"They were brutal to me."

"Did you ever see the Polish doctor after the operation?"

"No."

"But you are absolutely certain you can identify the man who operated on you."

"I was conscious the entire time. I will never forget the face."

"I have no further questions," Bannister said.

"No questions," Highsmith said.

"Is the inspection line-up ready?" Magistrate Griffin asked.

"Yes, sir."

"Now, Mr. Janos. You understand what a police identification parade is?"

"Yes, it has been explained."

"There will be a dozen men behind a glassed-in room, dressed in simulated prison clothing. They are unable to see into the room where we shall be observing. One of the men is Dr. Kelno."

"I understand."

They filed from the conference room, down a rickety stairs. Each man was still full of Janos's tale of horror. Highsmith and Smiddy, who had fought so bitterly for Adam Kelno, felt an unavoidable twinge of apprehension. Had Adam Kelno lied to them? The door of Barrack V had been opened for the first time giving a glimpse of its horrible secrets.

Nathan Goldmark's chest nearly burst. The moment was at hand for vengeance for the death of his family, for justification to his government. The orgasm of victory. From here, there could be no further delays. The fascist would be brought to heel.

Thomas Bannister took all of this with the apparent dispassionate calm that stamped his personality and career as a human refrigerator.

To the man who had suffered the most, it mattered the least. Eli Janos would still be a eunuch when it was over and it did not matter one way or the other.

They were seated and the room darkened. Before them was a glass-paneled room with a height marker on the rear wall. The men in prison uniform were marched in. They blinked from the sudden shower of light. A police officer directed them to face the dark room beyond the glass.

Adam Kelno stood second from the right in a mixture of tall and short and fat and thin people. Eli Janos leaned forward and squinted. Immediate identification eluded him so he started at the left side of the line-up.

"Do take your time," Magistrate Griffin said.

All that broke the silence was the deep wheezing of Nathan Goldmark and it was all he could do to restrain himself from jumping up and pointing at Kelno.

Janos's eyes stopped for a long search of each of them, probing for recognition of that terrible day in Barrack V.

Down the line. One, then the other. He came to Adam Kelno and hunched forward. The officer inside ordered everyone to turn left profile, then right profile. Then they were marched out and the light turned on.

"Well?" Magistrate Griffin asked.

Eli Janos drew a deep breath and shook his head. "I do not recognize any of them."

"Have the officer bring in Dr. Kelno," Robert Highsmith said in a sudden, unexpected flare.

"It's not required," the magistrate said.

"This bloody business has been going on for two years. A blameless man has been in prison. I want to make completely certain of this."

Adam Kelno was marched in and made to stand before Eli Janos and they stared at each other.

"Dr. Kelno," Highsmith said, "would you speak to this man in German or Polish."

"I want my freedom," Adam said in German. "It's in your hands," he concluded in Polish.

"Does the voice mean anything?" Highsmith said.

"He is not the man who castrated me," Eli Janos said.

Adam Kelno sighed deeply and bowed his head as the officer led him out.

"Are you willing to swear a statement?" Highsmith asked.

"Of course," Janos answered.

There was a formal letter that His Majesty's government regretted any inconvenience to Adam Kelno for his two year detention in Brixton Prison.

As the prison gate closed behind him, the patient and loving Angela rushed to his arms. Behind her, in the alleyway that lead to the entrance, his cousin Zenon Myslenski with Count Anatol Czerny, Highsmith, and Smiddy. There was someone else. A little boy who wavered cautiously under the prodding of "Uncle" Zenon. Then he toddled forward and said . . . "Daddy."

Adam lifted the child. "My son," he cried, "my son." And soon they passed down the long high brick wall into a rare day of sunlight in London.

The conspiracy had been beaten, but Adam Kelno was filled with an even greater fear without the protection of prison walls. He was on the outside now and the enemy was relentless and dangerous. He took his wife and son and fled. He fled to the remotest corner of the world.

7

"Adam! Adam!" Angela shrieked.

He tore over the veranda and flung the screen door open at the same instant Abun, the houseboy, arrived. Angela had flung herself over Stephan to shield the child from the cobra coiled near the bed, tongue flicking, head bobbing in a death dance.

Abun motioned Adam Kelno into stillness, slowly unsheathed his parang. His bare feet slipped noiselessly over the rat mat.

Hisssss! A flashing arc of steel. The snake was decapitated. Its head bounced off and the body crumpled after a short violent tremor.

"Don't touch! Don't touch! Still full poison!"

Angela allowed herself the luxury of screaming, then sobbed hysterically. Young Stephan clung to his mother and cried as Adam sat on the edge of the bed and tried to calm them. Adam looked away from his son guiltily. The boy's legs were still full of welts from leeches.

Yes, Sarawak in the northern corner of Borneo was about as far away as a man could run and deep as a man could hide.

A few days after his release from Brixton Prison and in a state of overwhelming fear the Kelno family booked secret passage for Singapore and from there a rotting tramp steamer took them over the South China Sea to the end of the earth . . . Sarawak.

Fort Bobang, a classic pesthole, stood on a delta formed by the Batang Lampur River. The outpost held a hundred thatched huts on hardwood stilts that nestled on the river's edge. A bit inland, the town consisted of two muddy streets of Chinese-owned shops, warehouses for the rubber and sago exports, and a dock large enough to accommodate the ferry that shuttled to the capital at Kuching and the long boats that traveled the endless rivers.

The British compound was a smattering of peeled, faded white-washed buildings scalded by the sun and beaten by the rain. In the compound was an area commissioner, a police station, a few banished civil servants, a clinic, and a one room schoolhouse.

A few months prior to the incident with the cobra, Adam Kelno had been interviewed by Dr. MacAlister, the Chief Medical Officer of Sarawak. Kelno's credentials were in order. He was a qualified physician and surgeon and men who desired to come to this place were not asked too many questions about their past.

MacAlister accompanied the Kelnos to Fort Bobang. Two male nurse assistants, a Malayan and a Chinese, greeted the new doctor without particular enthusiasm and showed him through the shoddy clinic.

"Not exactly the West End of London," MacAlister understated.

"I've worked in worse places," Adam answered tersely.

Adam's trained eye photographed the meager inventory for drugs and equipment. "What happened to the last man?"

"Suicide. We get quite a few of them out here, you know."

"Well, don't have any thoughts like that about me. I've had the opportunity. I'm not the type."

After the inspection, Adam curtly ordered a thorough scrubbing and cleaning of the building, then retreated to his quarters on the opposite side of the compound.

Angela was disappointed but did not complain. "A little touching up here and there and everything will be just lovely," she said, convincing herself least of all.

The view from the screened-in veranda was to the river and the docks below them back up to the hills that rose behind the town. It was all in low palm and an incredibly deep luscious green. As their drinks arrived, the sounds and smells of dusk invaded and a blessed blade of coolness cut through the wet suffocating heat of the day. As Adam stared out, the first drops of rain sprinkled down in prelude of the daily torrent to follow. The usual power failure of the compound's generator flicked the lights off and on, off and on. And then the rain came for fair, gushing and hopping off the ground as it hit with trip hammer impact.

"Cheers," said MacAlister. His time-wizened eyes studied the new man. Old Mac had seen them come and go, so many of them. The drunks and the dregs, and those filled with the false hope of bettering mankind. He had long forgotten his own missionary zeal, which was squashed by his mediocrity, the crown's bureaucracy and finally wrung out by the hot wet jungle and those savages down the river.

"The two boys you have with you are quite good. They'll help you learn your way about. Now that Sarawak has become a crown colony, we're going to have a bit more to spend on medicine. Spruce things up, here and there."

Adam stared at his own hands and flexed them and wondered. It had been so long since they had held the surgeon's tools. "I'll let you know what I'll need and what changes I plan to make," he said abruptly.

Rather a cheeky sort, MacAlister thought. Well, he'll get all that beaten out of him. He had watched them withdraw and grow cruel and cynical by the month, once they realized the unthinkable situation.

"A bit of advice from an old Borneo hand. Don't try to change things here. The people down the river will thwart you on every turn. They're only just a generation or two removed from being head-hunters and cannibals. Life is hard enough here, so take it easy on yourself. Enjoy our meager comforts. After all, you've brought a woman and child to this place."

"Thank you," Adam said, not really thanking the man at all.

Stinking Sarawak. Hidden from humanity in a corner of Borneo. It was peopled by a conglomerate of Malayans who were the Moslems and there were Kayans and the tribes of Land Dayaks and the Ibans, who were the Sea Dayaks, and, of course, the omnipresent Chinese, the shopkeepers of the Orient.

Its modern history came about a bit over a century ago when trade over the China Sea between the British colony of Singapore and the Sultanate of Brunei on Borneo increased to such an extent that it became a prime target of pirates.

The Sultan of Brunei was not only raided by the pirates but constantly plagued by uprisings within his own kingdom. Law and order arrived in the person of James Brooke, a swashbuckling English soldier of fortune. Brooke stamped out the rebellions and sent the pirates packing. As a reward, the grateful Sultan ceded to him the province of Sarawak and James Brooke became the first of the fabled "white rajahs."

Brooke ruled his domain as a benevolent autocrat. It was a steamy little state, with but a few miles of dirt roads. Its highways were the rivers which poured down from the hilly thick forests into the deltas of the South China Sea. It was a land blanketed in tropical foliage, inundated by two hundred inches of rain a year, and co-inhabited by crocodiles, rats, snakes, bats, and wild pigs. Its natives were beleaguered and decimated by leprosy, elephantiasis, worms, cholera, small-pox, dropsy.

Oppression was their lot. With pitiful little farm land, their meager crops were under constant attack by pirates and neighbors or taken by taxation.

They made war on each other and went into battle resplendent in feathered dress, and the head of the vanquished hung in the home of the victor. Those who were not murdered were sold into the slave markets.

Over a period of time, James Brooke and his nephew, who succeeded him as rajah, established some form of order so that one merely had to concern himself with the task of survival against the land.

The third and final white rajah, Sir Charles Vyner Brooke, ended the hundred and five year reign of his family after the Second World War. During the war the Japanese occupied Sarawak for its oil fields at Miri and when the war ended, Brooke ceded the state to the British crown and Sarawak along with Brunei and North Borneo became crown colonies.

Sir Edgar Bates, the first governor of Sarawak, was to take over a state that had grown to fifty thousand square miles and held a half million people. Most of these were the Ibans or Sea Dayaks, the former head-hunters of uncertain origin. Some say they were seagoing Mongols.

Sir Edgar, from the upper middle civil servants, did his best toward education and eventual self-rule. But all of those things passed over in the time of the white rajahs had taken its toll. The new Sarawak-Orient Company explored for oil and minerals and attempted to exploit the unending forest. Yet, progress was measured as the snail crosses the land and bogged in a quagmire of ancient pagan taboos.

When Adam Kelno arrived in 1949, he became the thirtieth doctor in Sarawak. There were five hospitals. This was the facility for a half million persons.

He was assigned to Fort Bobang in the Second Division of Sarawak, in the land of the Ibans, the tattooed head-hunters of Borneo.

8

Adam Kelno's boatmen deftly maneuvered the thirty foot thatched roof dugout over the bubbling rapids where the Lemanak tributary rushed into the Lampur River. It was not difficult to tell the doctor's boat for it had the largest outboard motor of any that pushed up the Lemanak. It smoothed and they glided past a brace of sleeping crocodiles. The sound of the motor sent them slithering down the sandbank into the water. A tribe of monkeys shrieked at them leaping along the treetops.

For ten miles up the Lemanak tributary there were a series of long houses of the Ulu Tribe of Sea Dayaks. Each of the houses was a communal village unto itself built on hardwood poles and housing from twenty to fifty families. The long houses running up to lengths of over two hundred feet hugged the river front. A pull-up ladder, once a defensive measure against attacking neighbors, served as a stairs to the common veranda. Facing the river, were a long uncovered drying platform and communal kitchen and work area. In the rear of each house there were small private rooms for each family. It was all roofed in palm leaf and shingles and beneath it pigs and chickens ran wild amid human feces, and mangy curs struggled for existence.

Fifteen such long houses formed a tribal unit of the Ulu's under the rule of a chieftain named Bintang, after the stars.

The arrival of Dr. Kelno's boat was greeted by the clap of gongs, the usual welcome for any visitor. During the day, as Dr. Kelno held clinic, the Turah's, the heads of the other long houses of the tribe, arrived for the council meeting that Bintang had promised the doctor.

By evening they had all assembled, bedecked in woven jackets of blazing colors, cone-shaped hats topped with feathers, and assorted arm and leg bracelets. They were olive-skinned men of five feet in height, with seminegroid features mixed with that of Oriental. Their shiny black hair was pulled back to buns behind their necks and their shoulders, legs, and hands bore heavy tattoo markings. Some of the older Turahs sported such tattoos awarded to a warrior for his kills as a head-hunter in days not so long past. From rafter beams, all about the long house hung dozens of heads, all scraped clean as the inside of pumpkins. As the Turahs gathered Bintang offered them hot rice beer and they drank and chewed betel nuts and puffed cheroots in a corner of the common veranda.

Beyond them on the drying deck, the women went about

their business of cooking, weaving rattan mats and bright cloth, making jewelry and curing the sago, a starchy food from tree trunks. Beneath their bare breasts they wore corsets made of many brass rings encircling the entire body and these adornments were decorated with coins and chain jewelry, and their ear lobes were deformed by heavily weighted earrings.

The mood of the Turahs, which had been lively, changed to somber as the dour Dr. Kelno and his translator joined them. Feelings about him were definitely mixed. Bintang bade them to place their highly colored and ornamented seat mats on the rattan floor. Dr. Kelno and his translator, Mudich, sat opposite them all. Bintang and his chief magician Pirak, the Manang of the tribe, sat off to a side. Pirak was one of the hereditary fakirs called by the spirits to administer health and the wisdom of the gods. There were numerous categories and ranks of the Manangs. Pirak, a wrinkled old specimen, was of a special breed known as Manang Bali, a male in female's dress and behavior. He was a seductress of young males but bisexual as well. Pirak received exorbitant fees of gifts and food for performance of his mystic hokum. Too old to inherit chiefdom from Bintang, Pirak was determined to hold his exalted position and felt that Dr. Adam Kelno presented a threat.

Meaningless amenities flowed and then the translator began the business, as the half-starved dogs snapped up the remains of the plates of delicacies.

"Dr. Adam say," Mudich began, "that monsoon season is almost upon us and river will swell. Dr. Adam not come back for long time. Last year during monsoon, cholera very bad. This year Dr. Adam wants no such. He ask to give medicine through needle to save from cholera. Only twenty families in all of the long houses agree. Why is this so, say Dr. Kelno."

"Because Wind Spirit, Sea Spirit, Forest Spirit, and Fire Spirit are chosen by the Chief Spirit, Patra, to rule over sickness. We have prepared birds to sacrifice and will beat gongs four nights after first monsoon. Tell Dr. Adam, we have many way to fight sickness."

"Many, many way," Pirak the magician added, pointing to his bag of omens, healing stones, and herbs.

A murmur of agreement arose among the Turahs.

Adam drew a deep breath, controlled himself, and leaned over to his translator. "I want you to ask Bintang the following. I will give my medicine to the families that want it. If, after the monsoon season is over, the families I have treated are all well but many others who were not given my medicine are dead from fever will that prove that the gods favor my medicine?"

Mudich pretended not to understand. Adam repeated it slowly. The translator squirmed, then shook his head. "I cannot ask such question of Bintang."

"Why not?"

"It will embarrass chief before his Turahs if you prove to be right."

"Well, isn't he responsible for the health and well-being of his people?"

"Bintang also responsible to keep the legends. Sickness come, sickness go. Legend remain."

All right, Adam thought to himself, I'll get at this another way. He once again explained carefully to Mudich the question he was posing.

"Dr. Adam say to Bintang, why is burial ground so close to river? Dr. Adam say it must be moved because it make water unclean and bad water cause sickness."

"No true," Bintang answered. "Spirit cause sickness."

Again the Turahs all nodded in agreement.

Adam saw the anger in Pirak's eyes. The Manang Bali was responsible for the disposal of the dead and burial was a source of much of his income and riches. "Legend say, must bury on hill rising from river. Burial ground in right place now. Must not be moved."

"Dr. Adam say burial unclean. People not buried deep enough and many without a box to put them in. This Dr. Adam say spoil water when it runs next to burial ground. Pigs and dogs no fenced so they come to burial ground and eat dead. When we eat pigs and drink water it cause sickness."

"If woman die bleeding when giving child, she cannot have coffin," the Manang Bali answered. "If warrior die he must be buried close to water to ease his journey to Sebayan."

"But when you bury him with all that food in the ground, the animals dig it up!"

"How can he travel to Sebayan without food? Besides, Dr. Adam, in Sebayan he no longer has trouble so is better to get there," Bintang said.

"If chief die," Pirak added, "he must be burned and given to Fire Spirit. Dr. Adam no understand we must bury depending on how someone die."

Moving the cemetery site now became another utterly useless pursuit. Kelno was being swamped under the weight of mysticism and taboos. He persisted.

"Dr. Adam say, last time he come he brought seeds and vines of okra to plant in field near sago tree forest. Bintang promise to plant okra because is good for us to eat and make us strong."

"We learn," Pirak said, "in omen from birds that fields by sago forest are cursed."

"Just how did you come to that?"

"Very difficult to read bird omens," Pirak said, "take many years learning. Way bird fly, way bird sing, way bird cry, way two birds fly together. Birds give such bad omen we slaughter pig in ceremony and read markings on pig's liver. Everything say fields are cursed."

"Dr. Adam say we have only half the farm land we need. We must make use of all of it. Okra will drive out evil spirits from the fields. Okra is sacred food," Mudich translated, as Kelno tried to use their own taboos to gain his end. But the frustration wore on.

"Dr. Adam buy four water buffalo from Chinese. Why you no go to town of Sarebas and bring back?"

"Buffalo sacred omen, like moth and blue bird."

"But you not bring them to eat but only to work with in field."

"Curse to make sacred omen labor."

After another hour of it, Adam was exhausted. He begged to be excused from the feast and the cockfight and tersely bid them farewell. Pirak, the Manang Bali, was now filled with kindness, having won all his arguments. Dr. Adam would not return till after monsoon. As he climbed into his boat and curtly ordered the boatmen to cast off, the Ulus on shore waved a halfhearted farewell. When the boat turned the bend, Bintang looked to Mudich and asked, "Why does Dr. Adam come here if he hate us so much?"

9

The closeness of the British compound at Fort Bobang imposed friendships on persons who would have spent a lifetime avoiding each other. Angela was particularly adaptable to the narrow social circle. Adam was not.

He had a particular dislike for L. Clifton-Meek, the Commissioner of Agriculture for the Second Division. Clifton-Meek's office adjoined his clinic and their homes were only separated by that of the commissioner, Jack Lambert.

The Empire was a haven that saved the mediocre from obscurity. Lionel Clifton-Meek was a prime example of the shoe clerk, the railroad ticket seller, the humbled assistant tailor who had wiggled his way into a niche in His Majesty's far-flung interests. It was a small hole to crawl into indeed, but once staked out it was his and his alone. Clifton-Meek carefully guarded against either taking on responsibility, or making decisions, or outside intrusions. He clothed himself in a blanket of paper work to expand a belief in his own importance. In this safe place he could wait it out and end up with a nice pension for loyal service to the crown.

If L. Clifton-Meek personified a low echelon of civil servants, his drab, turkey-necked wife, Mercy, even more vividly portrayed what was hated by the black and yellow people they ruled.

In England, the Clifton-Meeks would have lived a gray life in a brick row house in a gray town or in London in a walk-up cold water flat, where her only qualification to augment her husband's insufficient income would be to hire herself out as a maid.

But the Empire did much for the lowly of England. In Sarawak they had stature. In the Second Division there was no other agricultural commissioner. Clifton-Meek had much to say about the rice fields, and the rubber plantations, and spent much of his time frustrating the Sarawak-Orient Company by the endless chain of command. A bone in the throat of progress.

Mercy Meek had at her beck and call two Malayan houseboys, who slept on the veranda and chased after her with an umbrella to shade her milky freckled skin from the sun. And she had a pure Chinese cook. The artificial snobbery of their low ancestry caused them to hyphenate their name as a further gesture of self-importance. And to top it all, Mercy attempted to bring the God of the Episcopalians to these heathens. On Sunday, the compound vibrated with her playing of the organ and pounding the fear of Jesus into them to a response of listlessly mumbled prayers.

Commissioner Lambert was another sort. Like Adam's superior, MacAlister, Lambert was an old hand in these parts, a good administrator who calmly listened to the complaints of the native chiefs, did little about them, and saw that everyone was well supplied with British flags and portraits of the King for their long houses. Basically, Lambert and Kelno left each other alone.

But that time had to come when L. Clifton-Meek had been buggered about once too often by that certain foreign medical officer and filed an indignant report.

Before Lambert let the report go into channels, he thought a meeting ought to take place between parties. It commenced in the commissioner's boiling, peeling office under a tired overhead fan, which did little to bring comfort. L. Clifton-Meek's pinched white face quivered as he clung to the books of governing regulations while Lambert thumbed through the thick report.

Lambert mopped his wet jaw. It was a strange place for a man to perspire from, Adam thought. "It appears, Dr. Kelno, that we have a misunderstanding of sorts. I rather it not go beyond this desk if we can all reach an agreement."

Clifton-Meek arched his back as Adam glared at him with contempt.

"Have you familiarized yourself with Clifton-Meek's complaint?"

"I read it this morning."

"Not really a serious matter."

"I consider it quite serious," Clifton-Meek said in a voice that trembled with fear.

"What I mean," Lambert soothed, "is that there is nothing here that we chaps can't bandy about a bit and simply overcome."

"That depends on Dr. Kelno."

"Let's take a look here," Lambert said. "First, there's the matter of the okra fields proposed for the Ulus on the lower Lemanak."

"What about the okra fields?" Adam asked.

"According to this, it seems you recommended the planting of okra fields at the fifteen long houses under Chief Bintang, and you brought seeds and pods to them for that purpose."

"Guilty as charged," Adam said.

L. Clifton-Meek smirked and rattled his skinny fingers on Lambert's desk. "Okra is a malvaceous shrub, a planted crop that falls quite clearly under the agricultural commissioner. It has nothing to do with health or medicine," he bureaucrated.

"Do you believe that okra as an augment to their present diet would be good for their health or bad for their health?" Adam asked.

"I shall not be entrapped with your word games, Doctor. Land usage is clearly in my department, sir, clearly. Right here on page seven hundred and two of the regulations," and he read the long rule as Jack Lambert stifled a smile. Clifton-Meek temporarily closed the book filled with handy markers. "I am, sir, making a survey for the Sarawak-Orient Company for proper land use in the Second Division for the possibility of rubber plantations."

"In the first place," Adam said, "the Ulus can't eat rubber. In the second place I don't know how you can make a survey if you haven't once traveled the Lemanak River."

"I have maps and other methods."

"Is it your recommendation then that okra fields should not be planted?" Adam asked.

"Yes, Lionel," Lambert interjected, "just what do you propose?"

"I am only saying," he retorted, with voice rising, "the book clearly defines the duties of both our offices. If the medical officer just pops about taking matters into his own hands chaos will result."

"May I say candidly that if you were to take a trip down the Lemanak, as I have proposed to you on numerous occasions, common sense would show you there is no land available for rubber plantations. What you would know is that there is universal malnutrition due to insufficient farm land. And as for the rest of your ridiculous report only an ass would protest my purchase of water buffalos and recommending new fishing methods."

"The regulations clearly state that the agricultural officer is the sole judge in these matters," Clifton-Meek screamed with veins popping in his neck and his ruddy cheeks becoming crimson.

"Gentlemen, gentlemen," Lambert said, "we are all officers of the crown here."

"The crime I seem to have committed," Adam Kelno said, "is to try to better the lives of my patients and see them live longer. Why don't you take your report, Clifton-Meek, and shit all over it."

Clifton-Meek sprung up. "I demand this report be sent to the capital, Mr. Lambert. It is a pity we have to put up with certain foreign elements who do not understand the meaning of orderly administration. Good day, sir."

A disgusted silence followed Clifton-Meek's departure.

"Never mind, don't say it," Lambert said filling a glass with water from his carafe.

"I will make a collection of native omens, taboos, gods, spirits, rituals, and rules of His Majesty's Foreign Office regulations, and I'll call it *Handbook for Idiots*. The Meeks shall inherit the Empire."

"For some strange reason we've managed to muddle through for almost four centuries," Lambert said.

"Down the river they fish with spears, hunt with blow-guns, and plow their fields with sticks. Once you get an idea through their savage skulls there is always a Lionel Clifton-Meek to bury it in his paper heap."

"Well now, Kelno, you've only been out here awhile. You ought to know things go slowly. No use of all this tugging and hauling. Besides, most of the Ibans are nice chaps once you get on to the idea they have their own way of doing things."

"Savages, damned savages."

"Do you really think they're savages?"

"Well, what else is there to think?"

"That's rather strange coming from you, Kelno."

"What do you mean, Lambert?"

"We don't pry into a man's past here but you were a prisoner in the Jadwiga Concentration Camp. What I mean to say is, having gone through all that in Poland, done by an allegedly civilized people, it is rather difficult to really say just who are the savages in this world."

10

For the most part, Adam Kelno remained aloof of the small, stifling, repetitious, and dull clique of British civil servants at Fort Bobang.

His one meaningful friendship was with Ian Campbell, a craggy Scotsman who supervised a cooperative of small rubber plantations with headquarters at Fort Bobang to oversee the warehousing and shipping operation. Campbell was an unpretentious man, yet steeped in the classics and literature nourished during long, lonely seasons. He was a drinking man, a chess-playing man, a man with terse words and no nonsense for the pale colonials and of wisdom of the jungle and the natives.

A widower, once married to a French plantation owner's daughter, he was left with four small children who were cared for by a Chinese couple. He, himself, was cared for by a striking Eurasian girl in her late teens.

Campbell personally tutored his children with studies beyond their years inflicted with the zeal of a Baptist missionary. His own friendship with Kelno came into being when his children enrolled in the informal classes Angela taught the children of Fort Bobang.

His youngest son was Terrence, a year older than Stephan Kelno, who in short order formed a friendship that was destined to span their lifetimes.

Both Stephan and Terrence made remarkable adaptations to this remote place and both seemed capable of overcoming the disadvantages of their removal from civilization. The boys were like brothers, together most of the time and dreaming aloud of places beyond the sea.

And during those periods when Adam Kelno skidded into a tropical depression, it was always Ian Campbell whom Angela called upon to bring her husband around.

The monsoon season came. The rivers raged to impassability. And with it, MacAlister's prophecy of doom unfolded. In that second year, Angela had a third miscarriage and they had to go about the business of seeing to it that she could not become pregnant again.

Wilted by the heat and turned soggy by the rain and caged in Fort Bobang Adam Kelno took to heavy drinking. His nights were filled with a kind of madness, the recurring dreams of the concentration camp. And that nightmare he had known since boyhood. It always took the form of a large animal, a bear or a gorilla or an unidentifiable monster chasing him, entrapping him, and then crushing him. The spear or weapon he carried or his own strength was totally impotent in stopping the attack. As he was powerless to move, breathing became more and more difficult and al-

ways on the brink of death by suffocation he awakened
sweating, heart pounding, gasping and at times crying out
in terror. And the parade of the dead at the Jadwiga Concentration Camp and the blood of the surgery never stopped.

The relentless rain showed no pity.

Each morning he took longer to lift his head from the
pillow from the effects of alcohol and quaking after another night of horror.

A lizard flitted across the floor. Adam picked at his food
listlessly. He was in the usual bleary-eyed state of this time
of evening and his face showed a six day growth of stubble.

"Please eat, Adam."

He grunted an indistinguishable answer.

Angela dismissed the servants with a nod of her head.
Stephan Kelno was still a child, but he knew the reek of
liquor from his father's breath and turned his cheek as
Adam kissed him as he left the table.

Adam blinked and narrowed his eyes to get them into
focus. Angela, poor Angela, sat in sallow sorrow. There were
gray hairs in her head now. He had put them there with his
own paint brush of misery.

"I really think you ought to shave and bathe and make
an effort to come over to the Lamberts' and welcome the
new missionaries," she said.

"Lord God, will you stop trying to pawn off your only
begotten son on these cannibals? Missionaries. Do you really
think Jesus comes to places like this? Jesus avoids places like
this . . . concentration camps . . . British prisons. Jesus
knows how to stay out of trouble. Tell the missionaries . . .
I hope the head-hunters get them."

"Adam."

"Go sing your hymns with Mercy Meek. What a friend
we have in Jeeeeesus. Hail Mary. Mother of God. Keep
your nose out of Sarawak."

Angela pushed back from the table angrily.

"Get me a drink first. No lectures. Just a drink. Even
the goddam British gin will do. Aha, says the temperate
and long suffering wife, the one thing you don't need is
another drink."

"Adam!"

"Subject of the next lecture. My husband hasn't made love to me for over a month. My husband is impotent."

"Adam, listen to me. There is talk going around of dismissing you."

"Where'd you hear that?"

"Clifton-Meek was very happy to slap me with that news," she said. "When I heard it I wrote to MacAlister in Kuching. They are gravely concerned."

"Hurray. I'm sick of cannibals and Englishmen."

"Where do you think you can go after this?"

"So long as I have these," he said thrusting his hands before her face, "I'll find a place."

"They aren't as steady as they used to be."

"Where's my damned drink?"

"All right, Adam, you might as well hear the rest of it. I've reached the saturation point. If they sack you here . . . if you don't pull yourself together, Stephan and I will not go on with you."

He stared.

"We've taken all of this in silence and we've not complained about Sarawak. Adam, the one thing you've never had to question is my loyalty, and I'll stay here forever if need be. But I shall not go on living with a drunk who has completely given up on life."

"You mean that, don't you."

"Yes, I do." She turned and left for the Lamberts'.

Adam Kelno grunted and held his face in his hands. The sheets of rain plunged the place into darkness until the servants bathed it in swaying lamplight. He continued to sit to force rationality back to his fuzzed brain, then staggered to his feet and shuffled to a mirror. "You stupid bastard," he said to himself.

Adam went to Stephan's room. The boy looked from his bed half asleep and apprehensive.

Oh my God, he thought. What have I done? He is my life, this child.

When Angela returned she found Adam asleep in a chair in Stephan's room with the boy asleep in his lap. A storybook, worn from rereading, had fallen to the floor. Angela smiled. Adam's face was clean-shaven. He awakened to her kiss and silently and gently put Stephan in his bed. He placed the mosquito netting around him and put his arm about his wife and led her to the bedroom.

Ian Campbell returned from an extended stay in Singapore at a sorely needed time. He gave himself to his friend to bring him through a soggy brained monsoon rot. It came over long chess games, with children scrambling underfoot. After all, Adam came to realize, Campbell had done it as a widower with four children. And he found the iron.

"It's never so bad, Adam, that it's worth turning one of your children into a drunk or leading them to a life of darkness. After all, man, they didn't bargain for this place."

Adam Kelno decided he owed Ian Campbell very much and the way to pay it came through young Terrence. Often as not Terrence Campbell's curious brown eyes peered over the window sill of the dispensary, mouth agape.

"Come on in, Terry. Don't stand there like a Lampur monkey."

The boy would ease into the room and watch for hours as Dr. Adam, the magic Dr. Adam, made people well. As Terry's reward, Dr. Adam would ask him to fetch something or assist in some small way. And he dreamed of being a doctor.

When Dr. Adam was in a good mood, and Terry knew them all, he would ask a never-ending stream of questions about medicine. More than once Adam wished it were his own son, Stephan. But Stephan was outside doing something with a hammer and nails . . . a raft, a tree house.

"God works in strange ways," Adam thought, accepting but not accepting.

One thing was obvious and that was if Terrence Campbell had half a chance, he would be a doctor.

11

The monsoon season ended. Adam Kelno had returned to life.

A small surgery was installed with a capability of minor operations. MacAlister came from Kuching to attend the dedication and remained for several days. What he saw in the operating theater was a revelation. With Angela assisting, Adam performed a number of operations. MacAlister witnessed a complete change in Kelno with the surgeon's knife in his hands. Extraordinary skill, exquisite movements, command and concentration.

A short time thereafter the police station radio received a request from the capital at Kuching to have Dr. Kelno come to perform an emergency surgery. A light plane was dispatched to Fort Bobang for him. It soon became fashionable for the British colony in Kuching to have Adam Kelno as their surgeon instead of traveling to Singapore.

As soon as the river was passable, Adam headed up the Lemanak. This time his son, Stephan, traveled with him. He came upon the Ulu long houses to find that disaster had struck during the monsoon season in the form of raging cholera.

Bintang was in mortal grief over the death of his two eldest sons. Pirak had used water from sacred jars, magic oil, specially prepared pepper, and ordered gongs and drums beaten for days to drive away the evil spirits. But it came. Diarrhea followed by unbearable cramps and vomiting, dehydration, and the sunken eyes and fever and the leg pains and the apathetic wait for death. As the epidemic mounted, Bintang and those who were not stricken fled to the hills and left the sick to die.

The twenty families of the tribe who had taken Dr. Adam's medicine lived in six different long houses, and none of them fell to the sickness. Out of his own great sorrow, Bintang began to change his attitude. Although he still disliked the terse, cold doctor he now had to respect his medicine. Bintang called his Turahs together and with the disaster still fresh in their minds, they agreed to make changes.

The cemetery, a chief cause of contamination, was moved. It was a brazen step. Then, the long debated okra fields were planted and bullocks brought to plow the fields. The buffalo were able to turn the earth much deeper than their own crude hand plows and the crops of yams and vegetables became larger and finer in taste. Dr. Adam brought a fishing expert from Kuching who was able to replace the spear with netting methods. The chickens and pigs were fenced and the place to make human refuse was moved away from each long house. Much new medicine was given through Dr. Adam's needle.

And as the year wore on, Bintang noticed a change in Dr. Adam himself. In one way he was like the Ulu in his love for his child. With the young son and Terrence Campbell traveling with him, the doctor seemed much more kind. And on the second trip, Dr. Adam brought his wife, who also knew much of medicine and did much to take away the shyness of many of the women.

On the fourth and final trip to the Ulus before the monsoon, Dr. Adam's boat turned the bend to Bintang's long house and tied ashore just before nightfall. Something seemed strange. For the first time there was an absence of the greeting of gongs and a gathering of the villagers. Mudich, the translator, alone awaited him.

"Quick, Dr. Adam. Bintang's little son very sick. Crocodile bite."

They raced the path to the long house, climbed the notched steps, and as they reached the veranda he could hear low, rhythmic chanting. Adam shoved his way through the crowd to where the child lay groaning on the floor. The leg wound was covered with wet herbs and sacred healing stones. Pirak had chanted himself into a trance waving a pole topped with beads and feathers over the child.

Adam knelt and abruptly uncovered the wound. Fortunately he had been bitten in the fleshy part of the thigh. Some of the flesh had been torn away, the teeth marks went deep. Pulse, weak but steady. He flashed a light into the child's eyes. No serious hemorrhaging but the wound was dirty and débridement and drainage were needed along with surgery on a severed muscle. Temperature . . . very hot, a hundred and four degrees.

"How long has he been lying there?"

Mudich could not answer properly because the Ulus had no sense of hourly time. Adam fished through his bag and prepared a penicillin shot. "Have him removed to my hut, immediately."

Suddenly Pirak emerged from his communion with the spirits. As Dr. Adam gave the boy an injection he screamed in anger.

"Get him the hell out of here," Adam snapped.

"He say you are breaking the magic spell."

"I hope so. He's twice as sick as he need be."

The Manang Bali picked up his bag of magic potions, magic stones, tusks, roots, herbs, ginger, pepper and he rattled it over the child yelling that he was not finished with his treatment.

Adam snatched the bag and flung it over the veranda.

Pirak, who had been already disgraced by the cholera epidemic and with his power in the village slipping, realized he had to make a bold stand. He grabbed Adam's bat off the floor and flung it away.

Everyone backed away as Adam came to his feet and hovered over the old fakir. He controlled the impulse to strangle Pirak. "Tell Bintang," he said in an uneven voice, "the boy is becoming very sick. Bintang has already lost two of his sons. This child will not live unless he is given to me immediately."

Pirak jumped up and down and screamed. "He is breaking my spell. He will bring back evil spirits!"

"Tell Bintang that Pirak is a fraud. Tell him that now. I want him ordered away from this child."

"I cannot tell that," Mudich said. "The chief cannot throw out his own magician."

"This child's life is in the balance."

Pirak argued with Bintang heatedly. The chief looked from one to the other in confusion. Centuries of his society and culture weighed on him, and he was afraid of either decision. The Turahs would never understand such a thing as casting out his Manang. But the child. He will die, Dr.

Adam say. Ulus have uncommon love for their children. When his own two sons died of the fever he adopted two little Chinese girls as his own for the Chinamen often gave away the unwanted females.

"Bintang say, Manang must heal son in the way of our people."

Pirak thrust out his chest arrogantly and beat it with his fist and strutted as someone returned his bag of sticks and stones to him.

Adam Kelno turned and walked off.

Adam sat in naked futility under the waterfall below the river. He could hear the gongs and chanting from the long house. On the bank, Mudich and his boatmen kept guard for crocodiles and cobras. Poor Dr. Adam, Mudich thought. He will never understand.

He dragged himself, with weighted weariness, to a small separate hut that housed his clinic, and his own private room, which held a low palleted bed over the matted floor. He uncorked a bottle of gin and went at it until the sound of gongs and drums faded under the beat of evening rain, and then he stretched on his pallet and groaned to semi-sleep.

"Dr. Adam! Dr. Adam! Wake! Wake!" Mudich said.

With years of medical training he came awake instantly. Mudich stood over his pallet with a torch.

"Come," he said urgently.

Adam was on his feet, buttoning his shirt and tucking it into his trousers. In the next room Bintang stood with the child in his arms.

"Save my son," Bintang cried.

Adam took the boy and laid him on a crude examination table. The fever raged. It's bad, Adam thought, it's very bad. "Hold the torch closer."

As he set the thermometer into the child's rectum the boy went into a convulsion.

"How long has he been doing this. Before or after the sun?"

"When sun fall boy jerk around crazy."

That would mean three or more hours. He withdrew the

thermometer. One hundred and nine degrees. The child frothed and writhed. Brain damage! Irreparable brain damage! Even if he could pull the child through he would be an imbecile.

The little olive-skinned man looked up to the doctor with begging eyes. How to explain that the chief's son would be a hopeless idiot?

"Tell Bintang there is very little hope. He must wait outside. Mudich, set the torch in the holder and wait outside also. I will work alone."

There was no choice but to let the child go off to sleep.

Adam Kelno was back in Jadwiga Concentration Camp. The surgery . . . Barrack V. He leaned down close to the child and was compelled to untie the string that held in place a tiny cloth covering the boy's genitals.

IF THESE OPERATIONS ARE NECESSARY, I WILL DO THEM. DO YOU THINK I ENJOY IT?

Adam fondled the tiny pair of testicles, kneaded them in his fingers, ran his hand up the scrotum.

IF THEY MUST COME OFF FOR THE LIFE OF THE PATIENT.

He backed away suddenly and went into a violent trembling, looking somewhat mad, as the boy went into another agonized spasm.

An hour later, Adam emerged from the clinic and faced the anxious father and a dozen waiting tribesmen.

"He went to sleep peacefully."

When a primitive, as Bintang, emits the sounds of grief it is the cry of a wounded animal. He screamed and threw himself on the ground and beat upon himself in a tantrum of exquisite torment. And he wailed his hurt until exhaustion overcame him and found him face down in the mud bleeding from self-inflicted fury. Only then was Adam able to render him unconscious.

12

The police radio advised Kuching that the flying weather was marginal so MacAlister came to Fort Bobang by boat. He tied up to the main pier amid a small forest of dugouts, where Chinese and Malayans and Muruts and Ibans jabbered in a multitude of tongues in furious barter. Along the shore, women beat their wash clean and others drew water, carrying it in cans hanging from ox-like yokes.

MacAlister jumped ashore and walked up the dock past the main corrugated tin warehouse, where his nostril was pelted with the odor of slabs of freshly pressed rubber, pepper, and sacks of bat dung collected from the caves by the ingenious Chinese and sold as fertilizer.

The old Asian hand marched stiffly up the dirt road, past the Chinese shops and thatched huts of the Malays and into the British compound. MacAlister grumbled through a gargantuan mustache, as he slowed for his umbrella-bearing servant, who raced to keep the sun from his master's head. Knee-length stockings were met by long khaki shorts, and his cane popped in cadence to the crisp step.

Adam stood up from the chess game to greet him. Mac-Alister studied the board, then looked to Adam's opponent, his seven-year-old son, who was giving his father a trimming. The boy shook MacAlister's hand and Adam shooed him off.

"The lad plays quite a game."

Adam could scarcely conceal his pride in Stephan, who at this early age could read and speak English, Polish, and a smattering of Chinese and Malay.

After a time they settled on the screened veranda with the ever constant green view of the flowing rivers of Borneo. Their drinks came and soon the new sounds and smells of dusk invaded along with the blessed relief from the heat. Out on the lawn, Stephan played with Terrence Campbell.

"Cheers," said MacAlister.

"Well, Dr. MacAlister, what's the occasion?" Adam asked with his usual abruptness.

He laughed vaguely. "Well, Kelno, seems that you've

made quite a success in Kuching. Governor's wife's tonsils, Commissioner of Native Affairs' hernia, to say nothing of our leading Chinese citizen's gallstones."

Adam waited through the trivia. "Well now, why am I in Bobang, eh?"

"Yes, why?"

"To come right out with it, Sir Edgar," he said in reference to the governor, "and I have charted out an entirely new medical facility for the future of Sarawak. We want to move some of the newer men into meaningful positions as quickly as we are able to put the old-timers out to pasture. We'd like you to transfer to Kuching and take over as chief surgeon of the hospital. I think you'll agree it's becoming quite a good facility."

Adam drank slowly these days. He took it all in deliberately.

"Traditionally," MacAlister continued, "whoever is the chief surgeon is automatically assistant chief medical officer of Sarawak. I say, Kelno, you don't seem too pleased by all of this."

"It sounds very political, and I'm not one much for administrative work."

"Don't be so modest. You were the C.M.O. at the Polish army hospital at Tunbridge Wells."

"I never got used to filling out reports and playing politics."

"What about Jadwiga?"

Adam paled a bit.

"We're not pushing you up past a dozen men in the dark. Nor are we bringing up a past you want to forget, but your responsibilities were for hundreds of thousands of people there. Sir Edgar and I think you're the best man."

"It has taken me five years to get the trust of the Ulus," Adam said. "With Bintang and his Turahs I have been able to get many projects started and just now we are able to draw comparative results. I have become quite caught up in the problem of malnutrition. A surgeon you can get in Kuching, and the British will never be short of administrators, but I feel that eventually something important may come to light out of my work. You see, Dr. MacAlister, in

Jadwiga we had to depend entirely on what the Germans provided us to support life. Here, no matter how bad the land is and no matter how primitive the society, one can always better one's self, and we are coming close to proving it."

"Ummmm, I see. I suppose you've considered the fact that Mrs. Kelno would be more comfortable in Kuching. She could pop over to Singapore a few more times a year."

"I must say, in all candor, that Angela is as excited about my work as I am."

"And the boy? His education?"

"Angela teaches him daily. I will put him against any boy his age in Kuching."

"Then you are quite definite about turning this down."

"Yes."

"Shall we let our hair down," MacAlister said.

"Of course."

"How much of all this is your fear of leaving the jungle?"

Adam set his drink down and sighed deeply, as MacAlister found him at his source.

"Kuching is not the middle of London. No one is going to find you there."

"The Jews are everywhere. Every one of them is a potential enemy."

"Are you going to keep yourself locked up in the jungle for the rest of your life?"

"I don't wish to talk about it anymore." Adam Kelno answered with tiny beads of perspiration breaking out all over his face.

13

Stephan Kelno was the apple of his father's eye and an unusually gifted boy. Perhaps no single thing impressed the natives more than the presence of Dr. Adam's son on the river trips.

Adam stood on the wharf, steeped in sorrow as the ferry to Kuching pulled away, and Angela and his son waved to him until they were out of sight. From Kuching they would take a steamer to Singapore and then on to Australia, where Stephan would begin his formal education in a boarding school.

Adam was filled with more than the usual parental fear that something might happen to his child. For the first time in years he prayed. He prayed for the boy's safety.

To fill the terrible void, the relationship with young Terrence broadened. From an early age Terry spoke in medical terms and assisted in minor surgery. There could be no doubt that he would make an extraordinary doctor and to make this possible became Adam's goal. Ian Campbell was for it, though he doubted that a boy from the jungle could compete in the outside world.

Kelno turned his enormous energy to a series of new programs. Adam asked Bintang and the other Turahs of the tribe to send a promising boy or girl in his teens from each long house to Fort Bobang. This took a bit of convincing, for the elders, who had always lived communally, did not wish to give up any manpower. Ultimately Adam was able to convince them that with special training they would be of more value.

He started with fifteen youngsters who built a miniature long house. The first programs were kept very simple. The reading of time, basic first aid, and sanitation programs for each long house. Out of the first group two of the boys were sent to the Batu Lintang Training School in Kuching for more sophisticated schooling.

Within the year Angela was teaching them how to read and write English, as well as some nursing. Even L. Clifton-Meek got caught up in it and opened an experimental plot of land just beyond the compound. At the end of the third year there was a major breakthrough, when one of the boys returned from the Batu Lintang School qualified to operate a radio. For the first time in their thousand year existence, the Ulus were able to speak to and hear from the outside world. During the monsoon season, the radio became a godsend to diagnose and treat a variety of ills.

Terrence Campbell turned out to be the hidden jewel in the program. His ability to communicate with the Ulu youngsters made things happen that awed everyone in the British compound. As more sophisticated textbooks arrived, Terrence devoured them. Adam was now more determined than ever to qualify Terry for a top English college. Perhaps some of Kelno's zeal lay in the realization that his own son would never choose medicine. But there it was, Kelno the mentor and idol and Terry the determined and brilliant student.

Mass inoculation of Bintang's people reduced age old scourges. Bintang's long houses were cleaner, the earth yielded more, and there was a little more time to live with a little less pain. Soon, other chieftains and Turahs petitioned Dr. Adam to send children to Fort Bobang and the center grew to forty students.

The budget meetings in Kuching were always a hassle, but MacAlister generally gave Kelno what he wanted. It was no secret that the Sultan of Brunei wanted Dr. Adam as his personal physician and offered a lavish new hospital. After two years, he got his helicopter, which increased his movement capability a hundredfold. The Ibans made up a song about the wingless bird and the doctor who came from the sky.

All of this was but a grain of sand. Adam knew that given all the resources he could command and all the money he could spend, there was little that would really change, but each small step forward renewed the determination to continue.

The years passed by and the work continued. But what Adam Kelno really lived for was the return of Stephan on the summer holidays. To no one's surprise the boy was skipping ahead in his classes. Although he fared well in Australia, Fort Bobang was his home, where he could take those wonderful trips on the Lemanak with his father.

And then Adam received news that distressed him more

than he believed possible. MacAlister was retiring and moving to England. There had never been either intimacy or affection between the men, and he wondered why it bothered him so.

The Kelnos went to Kuching, where a farewell dinner was given for MacAlister and Sir Edgar Bates, the governor, who was departing for England to attend the coronation of the new queen. Sir Edgar would also remain in England and a new governor would be assigned to Sarawak.

Even in places so remote, the British knew how to conduct their affairs with flourish and fanfare. The ballroom was white with colonial uniforms and colored with sashes and medals.

There were a multitude of toasts filled with true and mock sentiment. Things were changing quickly these days. The sun was setting on that Empire where the sun was never supposed to set. In Asia, and Africa, and America it fell like a house of dominoes. The Malayans in Sarawak had picked up the cadence of the freedom wind.

As the evening reached its zenith, Adam turned to his wife and took her hand. "I have a surprise for you," he said. "We leave in the morning for Singapore, and we will fly to Australia to visit Stephan and perhaps a short vacation in New Zealand."

The long night of Adam Kelno was coming to an end.

14

The new governor was a persuasive fellow and convinced Adam to take the appointment as chief medical officer of the Second Division. With freedom in the air there was an urgent attempt to leap forward. The training of civil servants and upgrading the medical and educational facility took priority. Development of forests and mines by Sarawak-

Orient ran parallel to an infusion of new teachers, nurses, airfields, and ports.

In the Second Division Adam was able to remain in Fort Bobang but inherited over a hundred thousand persons, mostly Ibans with a smattering of Chinese and Malayans in the population centers. Adam had four doctors and a dozen nurses and assistants and of course Terrence Campbell, with primitive aide stations at the long houses. They were badly understaffed to cope with the range of diseases and problems, but he still had a higher ratio than the other Division Medical officers, who could only claim one doctor to every thirty-five thousand people.

His long suit remained the utilization of the land. There simply was not enough grazing land or farm land, so the threat of famine always lurked. Even as taboos were being broken he was unable to penetrate the ones forbidding the eating of deer and goats. It was the Iban belief that these animals were reincarnations of dead ancestors. Conversely he was unable to stop them from eating rats.

In searching United Nations bulletins and other works on the subject, Kelno became entranced by similar work in the new state of Israel. Although they were entirely different in make-up, Israel and Sarawak shared the fate of land shortage and acute deficiencies of beef and protein.

Israel had filled the protein gap with crops requiring very little land. Intense chicken hatcheries worked on a twenty-four hour basis. This idea was not suitable for the Ibans. The buildings required electricity to light them so the hens would lay around the clock. Also, the chicken itself was a disease prone fowl requiring a more advanced mentality to raise properly.

It was the second idea that caught Kelno's fancy, the artificial fish ponds. Israel had a consulate in Burma, her first diplomatic exchange in the Far East, and a number of Israeli agricultural experts were sent to establish experimental farms. He was sorely tempted to go to Burma and study the fish farms, but his fear of being recognized by a Jew overruled it.

He gathered the available literature and near Fort Bobang had his students build a half dozen ponds supplied with water from natural sources with simple canals to feed them and outlet valves for overflow. Each pond was stocked with a different variety of fish and cultured with self-perpetuating algae and plankton.

A half dozen years of trial and error were required to determine the most reliable and hardiest crop. A variety of Asian carp did the job along with imported New Zealand lobster, which flourished in fresh water.

And then came the years of persuasion before fish ponds began to pop up near the fields of the Ulus on the Lemanak.

My Dear Kelno [wrote MacAlister]

Not much is happening in Budleigh-Salterton. I am so pleased we have stayed in correspondence. It is difficult to believe you have been in Fort Bobang over a decade.

I have read your paper on the fish ponds, and your new experiments in grinding whole trash fish from the ocean as a protein supplement. May I say right off that I consider this one of the most dynamic possibilities to do something about the most pressing problem in Sarawak. I'm glad now I didn't convince you to come to Kuching to practice at the hospital.

I fully agree that your paper should be read to the British Academy. However, I cannot go along with your idea obscuring the authorship to that of an unnamed "research team." The paper should, and must, have your name on it.

Pursuant to this, I have traveled to London on numerous occasions and working quietly with old friends in Scotland Yard and the Foreign Office we have delved discreetly into the matter of your past unpleasantness with the Polish Communists.

We have even been able to extend our inquiries to Poland itself through our diplomats in Warsaw. The results are all quite positive. All the Poles who were in the embassy in London are long since gone, and since you now have British citizenship there is no request for extradition on war crime charges of any kind.

Furthermore, I have spoken to Count Anatol Czerny, a charming chap, and it is also his opinion that it is all water over the dam and you have nothing to fear.

I am pleased to hear that Stephan is doing so well "down under." Count Czerny assures me also that Terrence Campbell with his superior grades in special examinations and the fact you applied for entry several years ago will be admitted to Magdalen College. I think it is the most beautiful in Oxford, dating all the way back to the fifteenth century.

Dear Kelno, please look favorably on my request to read the paper in your name before the academy. My kindest regards to your charming wife. In friendship,

Yours sincerely,

J. J. MacAlister, M.D.

Adam reached the decision to allow MacAlister to read his paper without too much searching. He had traveled on numerous occasions to Singapore, New Zealand, and Australia without incident. His nightmares had all but faded. It was his love of Stephan that cast the deciding vote. He wanted to have his boy proud of him, and that desire outweighed his fears. He owed that much to Angela, too. And so the paper was read under the authorship of Dr. Adam Kelno.

These were the days of the new enlightenment, when it became fashionable for white men to ponder about the unproductive fields and life of squalor of black and yellow men and mass death by starvation. A conscience stirred far too late with far too little to save more than half of the world that went hungry. Adam Kelno's paper created a ripple.

As a pure scientist he had to resort to a method believed by many to be extremely cruel. Half the Ulu long houses received his medicine, fish ponds, sanitation programs, and new crops and farming methods. The other half went without these things in order to furnish the comparative statistics.

The higher death rate, lower longevity, and level of physical development and vitality dramatized the impact of his program.

The use of human guinea pigs was something the scientists did not like but understood. A secondary part of the paper that concerned the breaking down of ancient taboos particularly proved interesting to those who had struggled in the colonies.

The paper was widely published and acclaimed and became a standard reference for those teams of doctors, scientists, and agricultural experts who were wrestling with hunger throughout the world.

The best of it all was that no adverse reaction was heard anywhere to Adam Kelno's name.

Eighteen months after the paper, "Artificial Fish Ponds, and Their Effect on the Diet and Health of Primitive Peoples: Use of Ground Whole Trash Fish as a Protein Supplement: Comparative Diet and Vaccine Charts," an internationally manned UNESCO team arrived in Sarawak and made to Fort Bobang for a firsthand look at Kelno's work. A month later a report was filed that "United Nations funds and personnel should be committed to Fort Bobang to join the study."

Adam now looked forward to Singapore as a place for joyous reunions with Stephan. This was to be an occasion among occasions. Stephan had been accepted at Harvard and would soon be traveling to America to study architecture.

"I have news, son," Adam said, unable to constrain himself. "Mother and I have talked things over. Fifteen years in the jungle is quite enough. We are going to return to England."

"Father, I'm speechless! It's marvelous, just marvelous. Strange how it all works. Terry in England with you. Me in America."

"One doctor, one architect from Fort Bobang. Not so bad," Adam said with just a tinge of sadness. "The United Nations people really have taken things over at Bobang. In a manner of speaking, my work is done. The medical facility of Sarawak has more than doubled and a lot is going on. I'm pleased to say that when Sarawak becomes part of the Malayan State, Sir Abdel Haji Mohamed, the prime minister apparent, wants me to remain."

"They're no fools."

Stephan knew it was his father's dream that they be together and he didn't want to dampen the moment but inside him he felt he had to do his stint in some faraway place.

The Kelnos traveled from Singapore to Kuching in the highest spirits. The capital was something out of Somerset Maugham. Lady Grayson, the governor's wife, sent the Kelnos an invitation to join them at a formal garden party in honor of the Queen's birthday.

As they arrived at the governor's mansion, Lord Grayson met them and escorted them to the lighted garden into an array of the top government officials in their whites and the Malayans and Chinese, who would soon be administering the state. As they entered a hush fell over the lawn and everyone stared at Adam.

The governor nodded and the native orchestra played a ceremonial fanfare.

"What's going on, Lord Grayson?" Adam asked.

He smiled. "Ladies and gentlemen, refill your glasses. Last night I was advised by the Colonial Office that the Queen's Birthday List has been published in London. Among those chosen for honor to the Empire, Dr. Adam Kelno has been awarded the Order of Knight's Bachelor."

"Oh Adam, Adam."

"Ladies and gentlemen. A toast. To Sir Adam Kelno."

"Here, here!"

15

Oxford—1964

Beyond the limits of greater London, England and Wales are divided into several legal circuits and numerous times each year, the judges leave London to dispense justice in the assize towns.

The circuit system was founded after the Norman invasion in the eleventh century, when the kings began the custom of sending their justices into the countryside.

Henry II, the first great legalist and reformer, formalized the assize system in the twelfth century and the procession of rulers continued to refine it.

Such a system is possible because England accepts London as the seat of the royal power with one set of laws for the entire country. In America, for example, there are fifty separate sets of state laws, and a man from Louisiana would hardly want to be tried by a judge from Utah.

Several times each year, the counties are visited to dispense justice in the name of the Queen, where the judges try the most difficult and major legal issues.

Anthony Gilray, who was knighted and named a judge fifteen years earlier in the Queen's Bench Division, arrived in Oxford on assize.

Gilray had a commission in the form of a letter from the Queen, which bore the great seal, and he traveled to Oxford with his marshal, his clerk, his cook, and his valet. It was a time for pomp and ceremony. On the first day in Oxford, Gilray and a fellow judge attended an Assize Service at the cathedral, entering the church behind the undersheriff of the county, the high sheriff's chaplain, the high sheriff in military uniform, the judge's clerks in morning dress of tails, and then the judges attired in full bottomed wigs and ermine-lined scarlet capes.

Here, they prayed for guidance in the administration of justice.

The courtroom. The ceremony continues.
Everyone rises and the commission is opened. The sheriff,

chaplain, and undersheriff are on Gilray's right and his clerk on his left. Before him sits the traditional tricorne hat and the clerk, a portly and distinguished-appearing man, reads the commission naming "beloved and faithful counselors, lord keeper of our privy seal and the lord chief justice of England, most dear cousin counselors, most noble knights" in their full and lengthy titles.

The clerk bows to the judge, who places the tricorne hat on his head for a moment, and the reading continues that all who have grievances can now be heard.

"God save the Queen," and the court is in session.

In the rear of the court an eager young premedical student, Terrence Campbell, poised his pencil. The first case concerned a medical malpractice suit and would be used in his paper, "Medicine and the Law."

Outside the courtroom there was the milling of spectators, barristers, journalists, jurors, all adding to the excitement of the opening of court.

Across the street, Dr. Mark Tesslar stopped for a moment on his way and watched the scene and the line of pompous old, highly polished, flag-bedecked ceremonial automobiles lined up before the courthouse.

Tesslar was now a citizen of England and a permanent member of the Radcliffe Medical Research Center at Oxford. He was curiously drawn over the street and into the courtroom. For a moment he stood at the rear as Anthony Gilray nodded to the wigged black-robed barristers to commence.

Tesslar observed the eager row of students, who always were present at such cases, then turned and limped from the building.

16

Angela Kelno, who was born and raised in London, was the most anxious about the return and the most shocked. No sudden arctic blast ever chilled more deeply.

> AT FIRST, EVERYTHING SEEMED IN ORDER WHEN WE LANDED IN SOUTHAMPTON. I THINK I CRIED DURING THE ENTIRE DRIVE UP TO LONDON. ON EVERY MILE OF THE WAY I REMEMBERED SOMETHING AND MY TENSION GREW. AT LAST WE CAME TO LONDON. MY FIRST IMPRESSION WAS THAT LITTLE HAD CHANGED IN FIFTEEN YEARS.
>
> OH, THERE WERE A FEW NEW SKYSCRAPERS HERE AND THERE AND A NEW WIDE DUAL CARRIAGEWAY INTO LONDON AND SOME ULTRAMODERN BUILDINGS, PARTICULARLY WHERE CENTRAL LONDON HAD BEEN BOMBED OUT. BUT THE OLD WAS THERE. THE PALACE, THE CATHEDRALS, PICCADILLY, MARBLE ARCH, AND BOND STREET. NONE OF THAT HAD CHANGED.
>
> WHEN I FIRST LAID EYES ON THE YOUNG PEOPLE I WAS UNABLE TO RELATE. AS THOUGH THIS WAS NOT LONDON AT ALL. STRANGE PEOPLE FROM A WORLD I NEVER KNEW TRANSPLANTED HERE. SOME FRENZIED KIND OF UPHEAVAL HAD TAKEN PLACE. YOU KNOW, YOU RECOGNIZE IT QUICKLY IN ENGLAND. THINGS HAD BEEN SO STEADY BEFORE.
>
> MIND YOU, I'VE BEEN A NURSE FOR THIRTY YEARS AND I DON'T SHOCK EASILY. THIS THING ABOUT NUDITY IN THE STREETS. IN SARAWAK NUDITY WENT WITH THE HEAT AND THE COLOR OF THE NATIVES. IT WAS RATHER SILLY TO EQUATE IT WITH THE LILY-WHITE PALENESS OF ENGLISH GIRLS IN CHILLY, STAID LONDON.
>
> AND THE COSTUMES. IN SARAWAK THEY WERE BASED ON TRADITION AND CLIMATE BUT HERE THEY MADE NO SENSE WHATSOEVER. THE HIGH LEATHER BOOTS COULD ONLY REMIND ONE OF WHIP WIELDING SADISTS IN THE SEVENTEENTH CENTURY PARIS BROTHELS. THE WHITE THIGHS TURNED BLUE AND GOOSE FLESHY IN THE BIT-

ING COLD SO THEY COULD SPORT HEMLINES AT THEIR BUTTOCKS. WHAT WE ARE BREEDING IN THIS GENERATION OF ICY BACKSIDES IS A FUTURE HISTORY OF ENGLISH HEMORRHOIDS. MOST RIDICULOUS ARE THE CHEAP IMITATION FURS THAT DON'T EVEN COVER THEIR BOTTOMS. WITH THEIR SKINNY WHITE LEGS POKING OUT OF THE GHASTLY PINK AND LAVENDER BUNDLES. THEY LOOK LIKE SOME SORT OF MARTIAN EGG ABOUT TO HATCH.

IN SARAWAK, THE MOST PRIMITIVE IBAN COMBED HIS HAIR NEATLY AND KNOTTED IT. THE DELIBERATE ATTEMPT AT SLOPPINESS AND ANTI-BEAUTY APPEARS TO BE SOME SORT OF PROTEST AGAINST THE OLDER GENERATION. YET, IN THEIR MANIA TO PROCLAIM THEIR INDIVIDUALITY AND BREAK WITH THE PAST THEY ALL NOW LOOK AS THOUGH THEY HAD BEEN CAST FROM THE SAME MOLD. BOYS LOOK LIKE GIRLS AND GIRLS LOOK EXCEEDINGLY DRAB. RATHER AN OBVIOUS ATTEMPT TO LOOK UGLY BECAUSE THEY FEEL UGLY AND A WITHDRAWAL SO THEY WILL NOT BE IDENTIFIED BY SEX. HAVE EVERYTHING ONE BIG NEUTER.

THE FRANTIC DRESS OF THE MEN IN BELL BOTTOMS AND LACES AND JUNK JEWELRY AND VELVET ALL APPEARS LIKE A CALL FOR HELP.

ADAM TELLS ME THAT WHAT IS HAPPENING IN HIS CLINIC INDICATES A TOTAL COLLAPSE OF OLD MORALS. THEY HAVE MISTAKEN SEXUAL FREEDOM FOR THE ABILITY TO GIVE AND RECEIVE LOVE. AND MOST SAD OF ALL IS THE BREAKING UP OF THE FAMILY UNIT. ADAM TELLS ME THE NUMBER OF PREGNANT GIRLS IN THEIR TEENS IS UP FIVE OR SIX HUNDRED PERCENT AND THE STATISTICS ON BARBITURATE AND DRUG USERS ARE FRIGHTENING. AGAIN, THIS SEEMS TO INDICATE AN OVERWHELMING URGE OF THESE YOUNG PEOPLE TO WITHDRAW INTO A FANTASY WORLD, LIKE THE IBANS DID, IN TIMES OF STRESS.

I COULDN'T BELIEVE THE MUSIC. ADAM TELLS ME THERE ARE MANY CASES OF PERMANENT HEARING DAMAGE. THE GARBLED POETRY AND DOUBLE MEANING OF FILTHY LYRICS ARE FAR LESS COHERENT THAN THE IBAN SINGERS. THE MONOTONE AND ELECTRIC DEVICES ARE A

FURTHER ATTEMPT TO DROWN OUT REALITY. THE DANC-
ING AS THOUGH ONE WERE WATCHING PATIENTS IN A
LUNATIC ASYLUM.

IS THIS REALLY LONDON?

ALL THAT I WAS RAISED BY IS BEING RIDICULED AND
IT SEEMS THAT NOTHING IS BEING DONE TO REPLACE
OLD IDEAS WITH NEW ONES. THE WORST PART OF IT IS
THE YOUNG PEOPLE ARE NOT HAPPY. THEY HAVE AB-
STRACT THOUGHTS ABOUT LOVING, MANKIND, AND END-
ING WAR, BUT THEY SEEM TO WANT THE PRICE OF LIFE
WITHOUT WORKING. THEY RIDICULE US, BUT WE SUP-
PORT THEM. THEY HAVE POOR LITTLE LOYALTY TO ONE
ANOTHER AND ALTHOUGH SEX IS PRACTICED IN UNI-
VERSAL LOTS THEY DON'T UNDERSTAND THE TENDER-
NESS OF AN ENDURING RELATIONSHIP.

COULD ALL OF THIS HAPPEN IN ONLY FIFTEEN YEARS?
THE DISMANTLING OF HUNDREDS OF YEARS OF CIVILI-
ZATION AND TRADITION. WHY DID IT HAPPEN? FOR
STEPHAN'S AND FOR TERRY'S SAKE, ONE MUST START TO
LOOK AROUND FOR ANSWERS.

LONDON, IN MANY WAYS, WAS LIKE WHEN I FIRST
WENT TO SARAWAK. IT IS A JUNGLE FILLED WITH
STRANGE NOISES AND CUSTOMS. ONLY, THEY ARE NOT
AS HAPPY AS THE IBANS. THERE IS NO HUMOR TO IT
ALL, ONLY DESPAIR.

17

It was expected that Adam Kelno, having been knighted,
would have capitalized on the situation to build himself an
exclusive practice in the West End. Instead, he opened a
small clinic as a National Health Doctor in a working class
section of the Borough of Southwark, close to the Elephant
and Castle in the brick row houses near the Thames where

most of his patients were warehousemen, longshoremen, and the admixture of immigrants flooding in from India and blacks from Jamaica and the West Indies.

It was as though Adam Kelno did not believe his release from Sarawak and wished to continue his anonymity by living in modest seclusion close to his clinic.

Angela and her cousin walked themselves foot weary in that magic quadrangle bounded by Oxford and Regent and Bond Streets and Piccadilly now swarmed with hundreds of thousands of Christmas shoppers in the gargantuan department stores and the ultra little shops.

Although she had been back in England for more than a year the biting wet penetrating December cold bothered her. The hunt for a taxi was futile. Orderly lines waited with British patience outside the stores and at the bus stops.

Down into the tube.

The underground crossed beneath the Thames to Elephant and Castle and she made home by foot, bogged under a small hill of packages.

Oh, the wonderful weariness, the wonderful tempo of Christmas back in England. All those puddings, and pies, and sauces, and songs, and lights.

Mrs. Corkory, the housekeeper, unloaded her arms. "Doctor is in his study, ma'am."

"Has Terrence arrived?"

"No, ma'am. He phoned down from Oxford to say he was taking a later train and wouldn't be arriving until past seven or so."

She poked her head in Adam's study, where he was in the familiar posture of scratching away at lengthy reports.

"Hello, dear, I'm home."

"Hello, darling. Did you buy out London?"

"Almost. I'll help you with the reports later."

"I think this paper work for the health service is worse than the Colonial Office."

"Maybe you'll use a full time secretary. We really can afford one, Adam. And a dictation machine."

Adam shrugged. "I'm not used to such luxuries."

She thumbed through his letters. There were three requests for speeches. One was from the Union of African Medical Students and another from Cambridge. He had scribbled a note on each reading, "decline with the usual regrets."

Angela was against it. It was as though Adam were trying to downgrade his small measure of fame. Perhaps he had had his fill of blacks and browns. Then why did he choose Southwark to practice, when half the London Poles would have doted over a knighted Polish doctor. Well, that was Adam. In all their years of marriage she had come to accept it though the lack of personal ambition annoyed her, for his sake. But no pushy wife, she.

"Well we're ready for the invasion from Oxford," Angela said. "By the way, dear, did Terrence say how many friends he would be bringing?"

"Probably the usual contingent of homesick Australians, Malayans, and Chinese. I'll be the epitome of Polish gallantry." They exchanged a small kiss and he returned to his paper work, then threw the pen down. "By God you're right. I'm going to get a secretary and a voice machine."

Angela answered the phone ring. "It's Mr. Kelly. He says his wife's pains are coming every nine minutes regularly."

Adam was up quickly and out of his lounging jacket. "This is her sixth so she'll be right on time. Have him bring her over to the clinic and call the midwife."

It was almost midnight before Mrs. Kelly delivered and was situated overnight in the clinic. Angela had dozed in the parlor. Adam kissed her softly, and she automatically arose and went to the kitchen to heat water for tea.

"How did it go?"

"Little boy. They're naming him Adam."

"Isn't that nice. Well we have four infant Adams after you this year. In future years everyone will wonder why every male from Southwark was named Adam."

"Did Terrence get in?"

"Yes."

"Sounds rather quiet for five boys."

"He came in alone. He's up in your study waiting for you. I'll bring the tea up."

Terrence seemed stiff as they embraced.

"Where are all your friends?"

"They'll be down in a day. May I speak to you about something first?"

"You'll never make a politician. I've been able to read that grim expression since you were born."

"Sir," Terrence spoke haltingly. "Well, you know how it's been with us. Because of you I was a doctor at heart since I can remember. And I know how good you've been to me. My education and how close we are."

"What's wrong?"

"Well, sir, my father mentioned some little things about you being in prison and up for deportation once, but I never thought . . . it never occurred to me . . ."

"What?"

"It never entered my mind that you might have ever done anything wrong."

Angela came in with a tray of tea. She poured in silence. Terrence looked at the floor and licked his lips as Adam stared ahead, hands tight on the arms of his chair.

"I've told him you've suffered enough," she said, "and not to pry into things we want to forget."

"He has just as much right to know everything as Stephan does."

"I haven't done the prying. Someone else has. This book here, *The Holocaust* by Abraham Cady. Have you ever heard of it?"

"It's quite well known in America. I haven't read it myself," Adam said.

"Well, the damned thing's just been published in England. I'm afraid I have to show this to you." He handed the book to Dr. Kelno. A marker was in page 167. Adam held it under a lamp and read.

"Of all the concentration camps none was more infamous than Jadwiga. It was here that SS Dr. Colonel Adolph Voss established an experimental center for the purpose of creating methods of mass sterilization, with the use of human guinea pigs, and SS Dr. Colonel Otto Flensberg and his assistant carried on equally horrendous studies on prisoners. In the notorious Barrack V a secret surgery was run by Dr. Kelno, who carried out fifteen thousand or more experimental operations without the use of anesthetic."

Outside a dozen carolers pressed close to the window and with frosty breath sang out.
"We wish you a merry Christmas,
We wish you a merry Christmas,
We wish you a merry Christmas,
And a happy new year."

18

Adam closed the book and placed it on his desk. "Well, do you think I did that, Terrence Campbell?"

"Of course not, Doctor. I feel like a bloody bastard about all this. God knows I don't want to hurt you but it's published and hundreds of thousands if not millions of people are going to read it."

"Maybe I felt so strongly about our relationship I never felt the need to explain all of it to you. I suppose I was wrong." Adam went to the bookcase across the room, unlocked a bottom cupboard drawer, and took out three large cardboard boxes filled with volumes of papers, files, press clippings, letters. "I think it's time you know everything."

Adam started from the beginning.

"I think it is impossible to explain to someone exactly what a concentration camp is like or for them to comprehend such a thing could really exist. I still think of it in gray. We never saw a tree or flower for four years and I don't remember the sun. I dream of it. I see a stadium with hundreds of rows and each row filled with lifeless faces, dull eyes, shaved heads and striped uniforms. And beyond the last row the silhouettes of the crematorium ovens, and I can smell the smoke of human flesh. There was never enough food or medicine. I looked from my clinic day and night to an endless line of prisoners dragging themselves to me."

"Doctor, I just don't know what to say."

Adam recounted the conspiracy against him, the torment of Brixton Prison, of not seeing his own son Stephan for the first two years of his life, the flight to Sarawak, the nightmares, the drunken stupors, all of it. Tears fell freely down both their cheeks as he continued in monotone until the first light of day cast a gray pall into the room and the first sounds of movement of the city could be heard. The wet tires sung off the pavement and they were silent and motionless.

Terry shook his head. "I don't understand it. I just don't understand it. Why would the Jews hate you so much?"

"You are naïve, Terry. Before the war there were several million Jews in Poland. We had only gained our own liberation at the end of the First World War. The Jews were always strangers in our midst, always attempting to overthrow us again. They were the soul of the Communist Party and the ones guilty of giving Poland back to Russia. From the beginning it was always a life and death struggle."

"But why?"

He shrugged. "In my village all of us owed money to the Jew. Do you know how poor I was when I got to Warsaw? For my first two years my room was a large closet, and my bed was of rags. I had to lock myself in the bathroom in order to have a place to study. I waited and waited to gain admittance to the university but there was no room because the Jews lied about themselves to find ways around the quota system. You think a quota system is wrong. If there hadn't been one they would have bought every seat in every classroom. They are cunning beyond imagination. The Jewish professors and teachers tried to control every facet of university life. Always pushing their way in. I joined the Nationalist Students Movement, proudly, because it was a way to combat them. And afterwards, it was always a Jewish doctor getting the prime positions. Well, my father drank himself to death and my mother worked her way to an early grave paying off the Jewish money-lender. All the way to the end, I stood for my Polish nationalism and because of it I have been driven to hell."

The boy looked at his mentor. Terry was disgusted with himself. He could see Adam Kelno tenderly calming a frightened Ulu child and reassuring the mother. Dear Lord, it wasn't possible for Dr. Kelno to use medicine wrongly.

The Holocaust lay on the desk. A thick gray-covered volume with the lettering of the title and the author's name in red portraying devouring flames.

"No doubt the author is a Jew," Adam said.

"Yes."

"Well, no matter. I've been mentioned in other books by them."

"But this is different. It has hardly been published and already a half a dozen people have asked me about it. It's only a matter of time until some journalist digs it up. With you knighted it will make a hell of a story."

Angela appeared in a dowdy bathrobe.

"What am I to do," he said, "flee to some jungle again?"

"No. Stand and fight. Stop the sale of this book and show the world that the author is a liar."

"You're young and very innocent, Terry."

"Along with my father you're everything to me, Dr. Kelno. Did you spend fifteen years in Sarawak just for the privilege of carrying this mark to your grave?"

"Do you have any idea of what this involves?"

"I must ask you, Doctor; is there any truth to this at all?"

"How dare you!" Angela cried. "How dare you say that!"

"I don't believe it either. Can I help you fight it?"

"Are you quite ready for the scandal and the barrage of professional liars they'll parade into the courts? Are you quite certain the honorable thing to do is not to hold our silence with dignity?" Angela said.

Terrence shook his head and walked from the room to hold back the tears.

Much beer and gin were consumed by Terry's mates and many bawdy songs were sung and many of the world's consuming issues were argued with a righteous wrath reserved for the young.

Terry had a key to Dr. Kelno's clinic a few blocks from the house, and after hours his chums dispensed of other frustrations by love-making with numerous young ladies on the examination table and the overnight cots amid the smell of medical disinfectants. A minor discomfort.

Christmas came and turkeys and geese were devoured and each guest opened a modest but well-chosen and humorous gift. Dr. Kelno opened a number of worthless but sentimental offerings from his patients.

It all seemed Christmasy enough and the visitors were unable to detect the underlying tension. They returned to Oxford filled with the cheer.

Terry and Adam said good-by with reserve. The train pulled out. Angela slipped her arm through her husband's as they left the Victorian loftiness of Paddington Station.

A week passed, then two and three. The listlessness of the student was matched by the listlessness and short temper of Adam Kelno.

It was the longest period of time the two had ever been out of communication.

And he was filled with the memory of the dugout struggling up the Lemanak with Stephan at the tiller and Terry on the bow chatting to the boatman in the Iban language. How warmly the Ulus greeted the boys. It was during the summer holiday, when Stephan was eleven years old, Bintang presented them with costumes and made them a member of the tribe, and they danced with the chief wearing ceremonial feathers and "painted" tattoo marks.

Terry's bright eyes watched over the surgical mask as Adam operated. Adam always glanced at him. When the boy was there he always performed a better operation.

The hard days of clinic at the long houses would be over and they would all go to the stream and bathe or sit under a waterfall and they slept near each other, never fearing the sounds of the jungle.

All the rest of it flooded his thoughts day and night until he could no longer bear it. It wasn't only Terrence who filled his thoughts. What would happen when Stephan learned of this in America?

Sir Adam Kelno walked the narrow Chancery Lane, that artery of British law flanked by the Law Society on one side and Sweet and Maxwell, the legal publishers and booksellers, on the other side. The window of Ede and Ravenscort, Ltd., tailor of the profession, held its usual grim display of academic and black barrister's robes, unchanged in style since time remembered and garnished with a variety of gray barrister's wigs.

He stopped at 32B Chancery Lane. It was a narrow four story building, one of the few survivors of the great fires centuries earlier. A warped and misshapen Jacobean relic.

Kelno glanced at the registry. The second and third floor held the law offices of Hobbins, Newton, and Smiddy. He entered and disappeared up the creaking stairs.

ii/the defendants

The author of *The Holocaust* was an American writer named Abraham Cady, one-time journalist, one-time flyer, one-time ballplayer.

At the turn of the century the Zionist movement spread like a forest fire over the Jewish Pale of Settlement in Czarist Russia. Bent under universal suppression and pogroms of centuries standing, the groundswell to leave Russia found direction in the resurrection of the ancient homeland. The little Jewish village of Prodno sponsored the Cadyzynski brothers, Morris and Hyman, to go to Palestine as pioneers.

While working in the swamps of Upper Galilee on land redemption, Morris Cadyzynski fell prey to recurrent attacks of malaria and dysentery until he was taken to the hospital in Jaffa. He was advised to leave Palestine as one of those unable to adapt to the severe conditions. His elder brother, Hyman, remained.

It was usual in those days that a relative in America take on the responsibility of getting as many of the family over from the old country as possible. Uncle Abraham Cadyzynski, after whom the author was later named, had a small Jewish bakery on Church Street in the ghetto in Norfolk, Virginia.

Morris had his name shortened to Cady by a perplexed official trying to separate over a hundred "skis" who immigrated on the same boatload.

Uncle Abraham had two daughters, whose eventual husbands were not interested in the bakery, so it was passed on to Morris when the old man died.

The Jewish community was tiny and close knit, hanging together unable to shake off all the ghetto mentality. Morris met Molly Segal, also an immigrant in the Zionist movement, and they were married in the year of 1909.

Out of deference to his father, the Rabbi of Prodno, they

were married in synagogue. The party afterward at the Workman's Circle Hall was in the Yiddish tradition of an endless parade of food, dancing the hora and *"mazel tovfs"* until the middle of the night.

Neither of them were religious, but they were never able to break most of the old country ties of conversing and reading in Yiddish and keeping a mostly kosher kitchen.

Ben was the first born in 1912 and then Sophie came two years later as Europe was going up in flames. During the First World War business prospered. With Norfolk as a major troop and supply shipping point to France, the government gave Morris's bakery a contract to augment overburdened facilities. The output of the bakery tripled and quadrupled but in doing so it lost most of its Jewish identity. The bread and cakes had come from old family recipes and now they had to conform to government specifications. After the war Morris got some of the old flavor back. He was so popular all over Norfolk that he began to ship out to grocery stores, some in all gentile neighborhoods.

Abraham Cady was born in 1920. Although it was a prosperous family it was difficult to tear away from the little row house with the white porch on Holt Street in which all the children were born.

The Jewish section started in the one hundred block of Church Street at St. Mary's Church and ran for seven blocks to where the Booker T. Pharmacy started the Negro ghetto. The streets were lined with little shops out of the old country and the children were to remember the smells and sounds of it all their lives. Heated discussion in Yiddish where the two newspapers, the *Freiheit* and New York *Vorwärts* vied for opinion. There was the marvelous odor of leather from Cousin Herschel's shoe repair shop and the pungent aroma of the cellar of the "pickle" man, where you could have a choice of sixty different kinds of pickles and pickled onions from briny old vats. They cost a penny each, two cents for an extra.

In the back yard behind Finkelstein's Prime and Fancy Kosher meats the kids liked to watch the *shochet* kill chickens for a nickel each to conform to religious requirements.

There was endless barter at the vegetable stalls and at Max Lipshitz's Super Stupendous Clothing Mart; Max himself, measuring tape around his neck, pulled potential customers off the street and just a little ways down Sol's Pawn Shop held a junk yard of tragedy, mostly from colored customers.

Much of what Morris Cady earned went either to the families in the old country or to Palestine. Aside from the black Essex parked before the house there was little to testify to their nominal wealth. Morris did not play the stock market so when the crash came he had enough cash to buy out a couple of sinking bakeries at thirty cents on the dollar.

Despite their simplicity, their affluence caught up with them and after a year of discussion they bought a big shingled ten room house on an acre of land at Gosnold and New Hampshire Streets with a view to the estuary. A few Jewish families, upper-middle class merchants and doctors, had penetrated Colonial Place but further down the line around Colley Street and Thirty-first. The Cadys had moved into an all gentile neighborhood.

Not that the Cadys were black, but they weren't exactly white. Ben and Abe were "the Jew boys." The Hebes, Yids, Sheenies, Kikes. Much of this was changed at the big circle at Pennsylvania and Delaware, where they played ball near the pumping station. Ben Cady was handy with his dukes and a definite risk to provoke or attack. After Ben established an understanding to live by with the neighborhood kids they all discovered the never ending delights that came from the oven of Molly's kitchen.

Abe had to go through it all again in J. E. B. Stuart Grammar School, filled with youngsters from the nearby Turney Boys' Home, consisting mainly of problem children from broken families. All they seemed to want to do was fight. Abe had to defend some unknown honor until his brother Ben taught him "all the dirty Jew tricks" to acquit himself.

Fists gave way to a different kind of anti-Semitism at Blair Junior High but by the time Abe was a teen-ager he had a running commentary with the unpleasant aspects of his birth.

It was Ben who brought them honor by becoming a three letter athlete at Maury High by bombing baseballs out of sight in the spring, sharpshooting baskets and plunging for hard yardage in the fall and winter.

After a time the neighbors pointed with certain curious pride to the Jewish family. They were good Jews. They knew their place. But the strangeness of entering a gentile home never exactly wore off.

What Abe Cady remembered the most about his father was his devotion to the family in the old country. His restlessness to get them all out of Poland. Morris brought a half dozen cousins to America and paid passage for another half dozen to Palestine. But try as he might, he could never induce his father, the Rabbi of Prodno, and his two younger brothers to leave. One was a doctor and the other a successful merchant, who were to remain in Poland until the tragic end.

Sophie, the daughter, was plain. She married a plain guy with a promising sales route in Baltimore, where most of the Cadyzynski family had settled. It was nice to travel to Baltimore for family reunions. One couldn't complain. America had been good. They were reasonably successful and always close in a pinch despite the usual family squabbles and feuds.

It was Ben who gave Morris and Molly the heartaches. They were proud enough of their athlete hero son. Such glory he had brought them, they could not deny. There was a school cheer for Ben even after he graduated. BASH EM, BAM EM, BEN, BEN, BEN!

Ben Cady was a child of the thirties. He never saw a colored person without feeling pain for him. Sensitive to the suffering of the depression, despising the ignorance of the South, he leaned more and more to the clever and fanatic voices that promised liberation of the toiling masses. It made more sense to him than anything in the world. The Earl Browders and Mother Bloors and James Fords who came down from the North and dared preach their gospel in mixed meetings with the blacks in tiny black halls of black town.

"So look, son," Morris said to Ben, "you don't want to be a baker and that's fine by me. I don't want my sons to be bakers. We can hire a foreman, we can hire bookkeepers so there should always be income from the business. Don't do me favors. Don't be a baker. Ben, look already, nine colleges, including the University of West Virginia, are on their knees begging humbly to give you an athletic scholarship."

Ben Cady had black eyes and black brows and black hair, and when not bursting from his intensity on the athletic field it burst from his being in a manner that no one could fail to understand.

"I want to screw around for a few years, Dad. You know, just look things over. Maybe sign on a ship."

"You want to be a bum."

Abe turned off the Jack Benny radio show because they were starting to talk loud in the next room. He stood in the door, gangly. He looked about half the size of Ben.

"Abe, go do your homework."

"It's July, Pop. I don't have any homework."

"So you've got to come in and take Ben's side and gang up on me."

At this point Morris Cady went through the story of his youth in Poland and his struggle in Palestine and his continued struggle for the family. All of this led up to his wife, Molly, the finest woman God ever created and then came the children.

About Sophie, what's to complain? A plain girl with a plain boy. Only three years married and two gorgeous children. Such *nachas* I get from the grandchildren. Maybe her husband Jack is a putz but he's a good provider, and he treats Sophie like she's pure gold.

Abe, look at the grades he gets in school. Nobody in the entire family denies Abe is a genius. Someday he will be a great American Jewish writer.

"Ben," Morris bargains, "Ben, let's put *tochis afn tisch*. You got through school through one method, brute force. So, you don't want to be a baker. Honkey dorey with me. But with fifteen colleges, including the University of West

Virginia, humbly begging your presence for God's sake get yourself a degree. I'm asking too much that you should educate yourself?"

Ben's face radiated blackness.

"How do you think your mother and I feel when you go to that *goyim* airfield and do those crazy things in an airplane? Spelling out names in the sky with smoke. That's what we struggled to raise you for? Let me tell you, Ben, you should see the look on your mother's face waiting for your footsteps to come on the porch. Your mother dies every minute you're up there in the sky. Some consideration. She cooks the meal, and she says to me, Morris, I know this food will never be eaten by Ben. Look at me, son, when I'm talking to you."

Both Abe and Ben have their heads hung and wring their hands.

"What's bothering you, son?"

Ben looked up slowly. "Poverty," he said, "fascism, inequality."

"You think I didn't hear all that Commie crap in Poland. You're a Jew, Ben, and in the end the Communists will betray you. I know from firsthand what kind of butchers they are in Russia."

"Pop, stop picking on me."

"Not until you educate yourself. All right, son, it's fashionable for young people to go into the colored section and dance with *schwartzes*. First you dance with them, then you bring them home to your mother."

Morris held his hand up for silence before Ben could answer.

"Look at this business. Flying. Becoming a Commie, fraternizing with *schwartzes*. Ben, I don't have a prejudiced bone in my body. I'm a Jew from the old country. Don't you know I know how these black people suffer. Who, after all, are the most liberal thinkers and the most decent to the colored people? The Jews are. And if something goes wrong, if the blacks explode . . . who do you think they'll turn on . . . us."

"Are you finished, Pop?"

"Deaf ears," Morris opined. "I'm talking already to the wall."

2

WE DIDN'T LEARN ABOUT MY BROTHER BEN GETTING KILLED BY A TELEGRAM OR ANYTHING LIKE THAT. WE GOT A LETTER FROM ONE OF HIS BUDDIES IN THE LACALLE SQUADRON, A GROUP OF AMERICAN VOLUNTEERS FLYING FOR LOYALIST SPAIN. SOME WERE MERCENARIES AND SOME, LIKE BEN, WERE TRUE ANTIFASCISTS. IT WAS A RAG-TAG GANG. ANYHOW, IT SEEMED KIND OF STRANGE THAT THE LETTER WAS FILLED MORE WITH TALK ABOUT THE CAUSE FOR WHICH BEN DIED AND THE FACT THAT THE FASCIST FLYERS WERE COWARDS.

BEN WAS FLYING A RUSSIAN CHATOS BIPLANE. IT WAS OUTDATED AND THEY WERE ALWAYS OUTNUMBERED BY THE SWARMS OF GERMAN HEINKELS AND ITALIAN FIATS. ON THIS PARTICULAR MISSION BEN HAD DOWNED A JUNKER BOMBER, WHEN THEY GOT INTO A DOGFIGHT. THREE AMERICANS WERE JUMPED BY THIRTY-FIVE HEINKELS, THE LETTER SAID.

BEN'S DEATH WAS LATER CONFIRMED BY A GUY WHO CAME TO VISIT US IN NORFOLK, WHO HAD BEEN A VOLUNTEER IN THE LINCOLN BATTALION OF THE INTERNATIONAL BRIGADE. HE HAD BEEN WOUNDED AND LOST AN ARM, AND WAS SENT BACK TO THE STATES AS A RECRUITER.

ALL THE RELATIVES CAME DOWN FROM BALTIMORE WHEN THEY HEARD BEN HAD BEEN KILLED AND ALL THE OLD FRIENDS CAME FROM CHURCH STREET. THE HOUSE WAS FILLED DAY AND NIGHT.

THERE WERE OTHER PEOPLE TOO. SOME OF BEN'S TEACHERS AND COACHES AND CLASSMATES AND NEIGHBORS, SOME OF WHOM HAD NEVER SAID HELLO OR SET FOOT IN OUR HOUSE BEFORE. EVEN TWO MINISTERS, A BAPTIST PREACHER, AND A CATHOLIC PRIEST CAME TO VISIT MOMMA AND POPPA. POPPA ALWAYS GAVE DONATIONS TO ALL THE CHURCHES IN THE NAME OF THE BAKERY.

FOR THE FIRST TWO WEEKS MOMMA NEVER STOPPED COOKING. SHE KEPT SAYING OVER AND OVER THAT THE COMPANY SHOULDN'T GO HUNGRY. BUT WE ALL KNEW SHE WAS WORKING TO BURN UP THE NERVOUS ENERGY AND KEEP BUSY SO SHE COULDN'T THINK ABOUT BEN.

AND THEN SHE CAME APART AND HAD TO BE PUT UNDER SEDATION. SHE AND POPPA WENT AWAY FOR A LONG REST TO SOPHIE'S IN BALTIMORE AND LATER TO THE CATSKILLS AND MIAMI. BUT EACH TIME THEY CAME BACK TO NORFOLK IT WAS LIKE THEY HAD COME HOME TO A MORTUARY. MOMMA AND POPPA WOULD GO TO BEN'S ROOM AND SIT BY THE HOUR LOOKING AT HIS SCHOOL PICTURES AND TROPHIES AND READ AND REREAD HIS LETTERS.

I DON'T THINK THEY WERE EVER THE SAME AFTER BEN DIED. IT SEEMED THEY STARTED GROWING OLD THE DAY THEY HEARD THE NEWS. FUNNY, UP TILL THEN I NEVER THOUGHT OF MY PARENTS GROWING OLD.

SOME COMMUNIST FRIENDS OF BEN'S CAME TO OUR HOUSE AND TOLD MOMMA AND POPPA THAT BEN'S DEATH SHOULD NOT BE IN VAIN. THEY PERSUADED THEM TO ATTEND A RALLY FOR LOYALIST SPAIN IN WASHINGTON. I WENT UP WITH THEM. BEN WAS EXTOLLED AND THEY GLORIFIED MOMMA AND POPPA FOR GIVING A SON TO THE CAUSE OF ANTI-FASCISM. WE ALL REALIZED THEY WERE JUST USING US AND WE NEVER ATTENDED ANOTHER OF THOSE MEETINGS.

I GUESS MY BROTHER BEN WAS THE MOST IMPORTANT PERSON IN MY LIFE.

I REMEMBER SO MANY THINGS ABOUT HIM.

HALE'S UNDERTAKING PARLOR HAD THIS BIG BOAT THAT HELD MAYBE FORTY OR FIFTY PEOPLE. YOU COULD RENT IT FROM THEM FOR $15.00 A DAY AND GET UP A BIG PARTY AND CRUISE UP THE CHESAPEAKE. EVEN THOUGH I WAS THE KID BROTHER HE ALWAYS INCLUDED ME. I HAD MY FIRST DRINK OF WHISKEY ON ONE OF THE SCHOOL PARTIES. I GOT SICKER THAN HELL.

ON THE BACK OF OUR LOT WE HAD A GARAGE AND OVER THAT, A LITTLE APARTMENT. THE PEOPLE WHO OWNED THE HOUSE BEFORE US HAD A COLORED COUPLE LIVING IN IT. BUT MOMMA LIKED TO DO HER OWN HOUSEWORK AND ONLY HAD A CLEANING LADY ONCE A WEEK, SO WE USED THE APARTMENT AS A KIND OF HIDE-AWAY.

WHEN BEN WAS FLYING HE'D PLAY SEMI-PRO FOOT-BALL ON SUNDAYS AT THE OLD LEAGUE PARK FOR THE NORFOLK CLANCY'S. MAN, I'LL NEVER FORGET THE DAY HE MADE TWO TOUCHDOWNS AGAINST RED GRANGE'S VISITING ALLSTARS AND CUT GRANGE DOWN ON THREE OR FOUR OPEN FIELD TACKLES. BEN WAS REALLY SOME-THING. MOST OF THE KIDS DID THEIR NECKING ON MAY-FLOWER DRIVE ALONG THE LAFAYETTE RIVER, BUT WE HAD THE APARTMENT AND WE SURE HAD SOME GREAT PARTIES.

THE YARD BY THE GARAGE WAS PRETTY BIG AND WE'D FUNGO FLIES AND GROUNDERS TO EACH OTHER. USING THE SIDE OF THE GARAGE AS A BACKSTOP BEN TAUGHT ME HOW TO PITCH. HE PAINTED A TARGET OF A BATTER ON THE WALL AND MADE ME THROW AT IT UNTIL MY ARM NEARLY FELL OFF. HE WAS REALLY PATIENT.

HE'D PUT HIS HANDS ON MY SHOULDER AND TALK BASEBALL TO ME. WHEN BEN TOUCHED ME IT WAS LIKE BEING TOUCHED BY GOD.

"LOOK, ABE," BEN WOULD SAY, "YOU'RE NOT GOING TO DAZZLE ANYBODY WITH YOUR SPEED OR BLOW THEM OUT OF THE BOX. SO YOU HAVE TO PITCH WITH YOUR JEWISH HEAD." I WAS TAUGHT A VARIETY OF SLOW CURVES AND CHANGE-UPS AND A SLIDER. IN THOSE DAYS A SLIDER WAS CALLED A SCREWBALL. WELL, BEN TAUGHT

ME TO BE A REAL JUNK PITCHER WITH JUST ENOUGH
MUSTARD ON THE FAST BALL TO KEEP THE BATTER
HONEST. I WAS NEVER AN OVERPOWERING TYPE PITCHER,
BUT BEN TAUGHT ME ENOUGH TO BE FIRST STRING FOR
MAURY HIGH AND GET A SCHOLARSHIP TO THE UNIVER-
SITY OF NORTH CAROLINA. OFTEN WE'D PLAY TILL DARK,
THEN KEEP GOING UNDER THE STREET LIGHTS.

THERE WAS A DIRT AIRFIELD WHERE GRANBY STREET
CURVED AROUND THE BEND NEAR THE CEMETERY AT
DEAD MAN'S CORNER ON THE WAY TO THE BEACH AT
OCEAN VIEW. THE WHOLE AREA WAS IN TRUCK FARMS,
AND YOU HAD TO MAKE YOUR APPROACHES RIGHT OVER
THE TOMBSTONES. IT'S ALL PART OF THE NAVAL AIR
BASE NOW BUT ONE OR TWO OF THE OLD BUILDINGS RE-
MAIN. ANYHOW, THERE WAS THIS RICH JEWISH DEPART-
MENT STORE OWNER NAMED JAKE GOLDSTEIN, WHO WAS
A BIG FAN OF BEN'S AND OWNED A COUPLE OF AIR-
PLANES, ONE A WACO TAPERWING. IT COULD SHAKE
YOUR TEETH OUT BUT COULD YOU EVER DO STUNTS IN
IT. BEN STARTED FLYING THE WACO, AND I STARTED
HANGING AROUND THE FIELD.

BEN WAS THE ONLY JEWISH PILOT EXCEPT FOR MR.
GOLDSTEIN BUT EVERYONE RESPECTED HIM. HE WAS A
LOT LIKE THEM. YOU KNOW, A BREED APART SO BEING
JEWISH DIDN'T MATTER, AND WE DIDN'T HAVE TO GO
THROUGH ALL THOSE FIGHTS AGAIN.

JAKE GOLDSTEIN SPONSORED BEN AT A LOT OF AIR
RACES, AND HE'D GO OFF AND BARNSTORM AND STUNT
FLY AT FAIRS. WHEN HE WAS GONE I'D RUN ERRANDS
FOR THE PILOTS AND CHOCK DOWN PLANES AND THEN I
GOT TO TINKERING WITH ENGINES AND ONCE IN A WHILE
I'D GET MY REWARD, A PLANE RIDE.

BEN WOULD LET ME TAKE THE STICK AND LIKE EVERY-
THING ELSE, HE TAUGHT ME HOW TO FLY. BUT WHEN
HE WAS GONE SOME OF THE OTHER GUYS REALLY SHOOK
ME UP. I KNOW THEY WERE JUST CLOWNING, BUT
THEY'D START LOOPING AND SNAP ROLLING AND
WOULDN'T STOP UNTIL I WAS READY TO PASS OUT. I'D

STAGGER OUT OF THE COCKPIT AND RUN FOR THE TOILET AND PUKE MY GUTS OUT.

THERE WAS ONE ANTI-SEMITE IN THE CROWD. A GUY BY THE NAME OF STACY. ONCE WHEN BEN WAS GONE HE STUNTED ME UNTIL I FAINTED. SOME OF THE GUYS TOLD BEN ABOUT IT, AND BEN AND I QUIETLY WENT TO WORK. HE TAUGHT ME EVERY TRICK IN THE BOOK.

THEN, ONE DAY BEN SAID, "HEY, STACY, WHY DON'T YOU GO UP WITH ABE FOR A RIDE. I THINK HE'S ABOUT READY TO SOLO AND MAYBE YOU OUGHT TO CHECK HIM OUT INSTEAD OF ME." STACY FELL FOR IT. WE GOT INTO THE TWIN COCKPIT WACO, BUT WHAT STACY DIDN'T KNOW WAS THAT HIS SET OF CONTROLS HAD BEEN DIS-CONNECTED.

BEN GOT EVERYONE OUT TO WATCH. POW! WHAP! ZAM! DID I LET THAT SONOFABITCH HAVE IT. I FLIPPED HER OVER ON HER BACK AND BARREL ROLLED RIGHT OVER THE RUNWAY, THEN ANGLED HER UP SO STEEP SHE POWER STALLED AT THREE G'S RIGHT AT THE HANGAR. I LOOKED BACK. I THOUGHT STACY WOULD SHIT HIS PANTS. ANYHOW, I KEPT IT UP UNTIL HE BEGGED ME TO SET HER DOWN. THEN I LET HIM HAVE A LITTLE MORE, A FEW OUTSIDE LOOPS.

STACY NEVER CAME BACK TO THE AIRSTRIP AGAIN.

I WAS THE YOUNGEST FLYER OF THE GANG AND EVERY-THING WAS GOING FINE UNTIL I HAD TO DO A BELLY LANDING IN A CORNFIELD ONE DAY WHEN THE ENGINE QUIT. I WASN'T SCARED ALL THE WAY IN UNTIL THE PLANE STOPPED DEAD AND NOSED OVER. I GOT SCARED WHEN I CLIMBED OUT AND STARTED CRYING, "PLEASE DON'T TELL MOMMA AND POPPA."

I WAS BANGED UP REAL GOOD AND TOLD A WHOPPING LIE ABOUT FALLING OFF THE ROOF OF THE GARAGE, BUT THEY LEARNED THE TRUTH FROM AN INSURANCE AD-JUSTER AND INVESTIGATORS.

JESUS, WAS POPPA MAD!

"IF YOU WANT TO BREAK YOUR GOD DAMNED NECK, BEN, THAT'S FINE BY ME, BUT WHEN YOU TAKE A SENSI-TIVE CHILD LIKE ABE AND MAKE A GANGSTER OUT OF HIM, I'M GOING TO FORBID IT!"

MY POPPA, GOD REST HIS SOUL, HARDLY EVER FORBID ANYTHING IN HIS LIFE. HIS WAS THE FIRST BAKERY TO UNIONIZE WITHOUT A STRIKE OR BLOODSHED JUST BECAUSE HE WAS A LIBERAL THINKER. THE OTHER BAKERY OWNERS WERE READY TO LYNCH HIM, BUT POPPA DIDN'T SCARE EASILY. AND HE WAS THE FIRST TO HIRE A COLORED BAKER. A LOT OF PEOPLE MIGHT FORGET ABOUT HOW MUCH GUTS IT TOOK TO DO THAT IN THOSE DAYS.

WELL, I DIDN'T FLY FOR A LONG TIME AFTER THAT. NOT UNTIL BEN GOT KILLED IN SPAIN. THEN I HAD TO FLY AND POPPA UNDERSTOOD.

I GUESS WHAT I REMEMBER MOST ABOUT MY BROTHER BEN WERE THOSE QUIET DAYS WE JUST HORSED AROUND. MAYBE WE'D GO TO THE MARSH BEHIND J. E. B. STUART SCHOOL AND CATCH A COUPLE OF FROGS. THERE WOULD ALWAYS BE KIDS FROM THE TURNEY HOME THERE AND WE'D HAVE FROG RACES . . . OR MAYBE WE'D BOWL A FEW GAMES OF DUCKPINS AT THE OLD BUSH STREET ALLEY. IT WAS THE ONE THING I WAS BETTER AT THAN BEN.

BEST OF ALL WERE THE TIMES AROUND THE CREEK. WE'D GET UP EARLY IN THE MORNING AND TAKE OUR BICYCLES DOWN TO THE DOCKS AND BUY US A WATERMELON FOR A NICKEL. THEY SOLD THEM TO THE KIDS CHEAP BECAUSE THEY HAD SPLIT IN SHIPMENT.

THEN WE'D BIKE TO THE CREEK. I HAD MY DOG IN THE FRONT BASKET AND BEN CARRIED THE WATERMELON IN HIS. WE'D SIT ON THE BANK AND PUT THE WATERMELON IN TO COOL IT AND WHILE IT WAS COOLING WE'D WALK TO A SMALL PIER AND FISH FOR SOFT SHELL CRABS. WE'D TIE A PIECE OF ROTTEN OLD MEAT ON A STRING AND HOLD IT RIGHT ON THE TOP OF THE WATER AND WHEN A CRAB WENT FOR IT, BEN WOULD SWOOP IT UP WITH A NET. THOSE CRABS WERE PRETTY DUMB.

MOMMA DIDN'T KEEP A KOSHER KITCHEN, BUT SHE WOULDN'T LET US BRING CRABS HOME SO WE'D COOK THEM ON THE BANK WITH A PIECE OF CORN OR A POTATO AND WE'D HAVE THE WATERMELON AS DESSERT AND JUST LIE IN THE GRASS AND LOOK AT THE SKY AND TALK THINGS OVER.

WE TALKED A LOT OF BASEBALL. THAT WAS LONG BE-
FORE BEN STARTED FLYING. BETWEEN US WE KNEW THE
BATTING AVERAGE OF EVERY PLAYER IN THE MAJOR
LEAGUES. THEY REALLY HAD BALLPLAYERS THEN. JIMMY
FOXX AND CARL HUBBELL WERE MY IDOLS. MAYBE BEN
WOULD READ A STORY I WAS WRITING.

WELL, WE ALWAYS ATE SO MUCH WE GOT BELLY-
ACHES, AND MOMMA WOULD RAISE HELL BECAUSE WE
COULDN'T EAT DINNER.

EVEN WHEN WE GOT OLDER WE'D ALWAYS LIKE TO
WANDER DOWN TO THE CREEK TOGETHER. THAT WAS
THE FIRST TIME BEN TOLD ME HE WAS GOING TO BE A
COMMUNIST.

"IT'S SOMETHING POPPA WILL NEVER UNDERSTAND.
HE DID THINGS HIS WAY WHEN HE WAS A KID. HE LEFT
HOME TO WORK IN THE SWAMPS IN PALESTINE. WELL, I
CAN'T DO THINGS THE WAY HE DID THEM."

BEN HURT FOR THE COLORED PEOPLE, AND HE FELT
COMMUNISM WAS THE ONLY ANSWER. HE USED TO
TALK ABOUT THE DAY THEY WOULD HAVE EQUALITY,
AND GUYS LIKE JOSH GIBSON AND SATCHEL PAIGE WOULD
BE PLAYING IN THE MAJORS AND THERE WOULD BE COL-
ORED SALES PEOPLE AT RICE'S AND SMITH AND WELTON'S
DEPARTMENT STORES, AND THEY'D BE ABLE TO EAT IN
THE SAME RESTAURANTS AND NOT HAVE TO RIDE ON THE
BACK OF THE BUS, AND THEIR KIDS WOULD BE ABLE TO
GO TO WHITE SCHOOLS, AND THEY'D BE ABLE TO LIVE IN
WHITE NEIGHBORHOODS. IN THE MIDDLE OF THE NINE-
TEEN THIRTIES, BEN'S DREAMS SEEMED PRETTY HARD TO
BELIEVE.

I REMEMBER THE LAST TIME I SAW BEN.

HE LEANED OVER MY BED AND TAPPED ME ON THE
SHOULDER, THEN HELD HIS FINGER TO HIS LIPS, AND HE
WHISPERED SO AS NOT TO WAKE UP MOMMA AND POPPA.

"I'M GOING AWAY, ABE."

I WAS HALF ASLEEP AND GROGGY AND DIDN'T UNDER-
STAND AT FIRST. I THOUGHT HE WAS GOING ON A FLYING
TRIP. "WHERE YOU GOING?"

"YOU'VE GOT TO KEEP IT A SECRET."

"SURE."

"I'M GOING TO SPAIN."

"TO SPAIN?"

"TO FIGHT FRANCO. I'M GOING TO FLY FOR THE LOY-ALISTS."

I GUESS I BEGAN TO CRY. BEN SAT ON THE EDGE OF THE BED AND HUGGED ME. "REMEMBER SOME OF THE THINGS I TAUGHT YOU AND MAYBE THEY'LL HELP YOU GET ALONG. BUT MAINLY, POPPA IS RIGHT. YOU STICK TO YOUR WRITING."

"I DON'T WANT YOU TO GO, BEN."

"I'VE GOT TO, ABE. I'VE GOT TO DO SOMETHING ABOUT ALL THIS."

STRANGE, ISN'T IT? I WASN'T ABLE TO CRY AFTER BEN'S DEATH. I WANTED TO, BUT I COULDN'T. THAT HAPPENED MUCH LATER, WHEN I DECIDED TO WRITE A BOOK ABOUT MY BROTHER BEN.

I TOOK THE SCHOLARSHIP TO THE UNIVERSITY OF NORTH CAROLINA BECAUSE OF THEIR JOURNALISM COL-LEGE, AND THOMAS WOLFE AND ALL THE OTHER WRIT-ERS, REALIZING TWO OF MY AMBITIONS, TO WRITE AND TO PLAY BALL. CHAPEL HILL HAD THE MOST BEAUTIFUL CAMPUS YOU COULD IMAGINE.

I WAS THE ONLY JEWISH BALLPLAYER ON THE FRESH-MAN TEAM AND YOU'VE GOT TO KNOW SOMEONE WAS ALWAYS TRYING TO STICK A FAST BALL IN MY EAR OR CUT ME IN HALF WITH THEIR SPIKES.

THE TEAM COACH WAS A WASHED-OUT RED NECK, WHO NEVER GOT HIGHER THAN THE B LEAGUES AND EVEN CHAWED HIS TOBACCO LIKE A BUSHER. HE DIDN'T LIKE ME. HE NEVER MADE ANY ANTI-SEMITIC REMARKS TO MY FACE BUT THE WAY HE SAID, "ABIE," WAS ENOUGH. I WAS THE BUTT OF ALL THE LOCKER ROOM JOKES AND HEARD THEIR CRUEL REMARKS SUPPOSEDLY OUT OF EARSHOT.

I WAS THE BEST FRESHMAN PITCHER IN THE CON-FERENCE, AND WHEN THEY ALL LEARNED I COULD HAN-DLE MYSELF OFF AND ON THE FIELD, THANKS TO BEN, I

STARTED GETTING ALONG. EVEN THAT SONOFABITCH OF A COACH KNEW HE'D BETTER TREAT ME TENDER BECAUSE WITHOUT ME THAT BUNCH OF MACKERELS WOULD BE AT THE BOTTOM OF THE STANDINGS.

THE TEAM HUSTLED FOR ME BUT IT WAS THE OPPOSITION THAT GOT TO ME. YOU SEE, I LOOKED EASY TO HIT, BUT I WASN'T. I PLAYED SOME PRETTY GOOD SEMI-PRO BALL IN NORFOLK AGAINST A LOT OF GUYS WHO HAD ONCE BEEN PROFESSIONAL PLAYERS AND HELL, THESE COLLEGE FRESHMEN WERE A BUNCH OF WILD ASS SWINGERS ALWAYS SHOOTING FOR THE FENCES. THEY CROAKED WITH FRUSTRATION, WHEN THEY COULDN'T HIT MY JUNK AND SOFT STUFF. AFTER I SAW THEM SWING A COUPLE OF TIMES I USUALLY HAD THEM EATING OUT OF MY HAND.

ANYHOW, MY HEAD BECAME THE BIGGEST TARGET IN THE CONFERENCE. IN THE FIRST FOUR GAMES—I WON THEM ALL BY SHUTOUTS—I WAS HIT BY OPPOSING PITCHERS SIX TIMES. FORTUNATELY I CAUGHT THEM ALL IN THE LEGS AND RIBS. BUT NONE OF THEM COULD MAKE ME BACK AWAY AT THE PLATE. I GUESS YOU MIGHT SAY I DARED THEM TO HIT ME.

"ABIE," OLD RED NECK SAID, "YOU'RE A RIGHT HANDED PITCHER AND A LEFT HANDED HITTER. WHEN YOU CROWD THE PLATE YOU'RE EXPOSING YOUR PITCHING ARM. I DON'T WANT YOU TO BE NO HERO. DON'T CROWD THE PLATE. YOU'RE BEING PAID TO PITCH, NOT HIT."

HELL, I KNOW I WAS A BANJO HITTER. LOUD SINGLES AND AN OCCASIONAL DOUBLE, BUT I HUNG IN THERE. I GUESS IT HAD TO HAPPEN. ONE DAY A STRONG BACKED SCATTER-ARMED LEFTY FROM DUKE CAUGHT ME WITH A BLAZER RIGHT ABOVE MY ELBOW AND BUSTED IT.

WHEN I CAME OUT OF THE CAST, I EXERCISED UNTIL I CRIED. THE DAMAGE WASN'T PERMANENT, BUT I COULDN'T REGAIN MY PIN POINT CONTROL. ALL THOSE BALLS I THREW AT THE GARAGE DOOR, ALL THE DAYS OF CATCH WITH BEN WERE DOWN THE DRAIN. THE ATHLETIC DEPARTMENT KINDLY INFORMED ME THAT MY SCHOLARSHIP WASN'T AVAILABLE ANY LONGER.

POPPA WANTED ME TO STAY IN COLLEGE, BUT I WAS GETTING THE FEELING THAT YOU CAN'T LEARN TO WRITE FROM COLLEGE PROFESSORS. ESPECIALLY PROFESSORS WHO DIDN'T KNOW MY BROTHER BEN, OR ANYTHING ABOUT THE THINGS I WANTED TO WRITE. AND MY BASEBALL CAREER WAS OVER, WHICH WAS NO GREAT LOSS.

I QUIT AFTER MY FRESHMAN YEAR AND AFTER NAGGING A LOT OF NEWSPAPERS I WAS HIRED BY THE VIRGINIA PILOT AS THE AVIATION EDITOR AT THIRTY BUCKS A WEEK. AT NIGHT I WROTE FOR THE PULP MAGAZINES LIKE "DOC SAVAGE" AND "DIME WESTERN" FOR A PENNY A WORD UNDER THE NAME OF HORACE ABRAHAM.

AND THEN ONE DAY I GOT TIRED OF THE PULPS AND BEGAN TO WORK ON MY NOVEL, THE ONE ABOUT BEN.

3

David Shawcross was more than a publisher. He was an editor of near legendary proportions running what was tantamount to a one-man house. He had emerged from the ranks of the English publishing dynasty, starting as errand boy at five shillings a week and working up to editor in chief over a period of two decades.

When he was twenty-one Shawcross headed the popular publication division for the notable sum of thirty shillings a week. In order to exist he deviled on the side synopsizing incoming manuscripts for other publishers.

David Shawcross survived all of this through sheer brilliant editorial talent. He refused to become a company henchman although named to the board.

Shawcross quit at a time of his own choosing and began his own small publishing firm.

Shawcross rarely published more than a dozen books a

year but each carried a special merit and it seemed that once
a year one of his books dented the best seller lists. Good
writers were attracted to the house because of its quality
reputation and the desire to have David Shawcross as their
editor.

As a small publisher he had to stay afloat through new
talent, which not only required sharp instincts but endless
digging. Americans were the most popular writers in the
world, but he was unable to bid against the large British
firms for them. He did it in another way.

By astute analysis he knew that the major American
editors ran on a treadmill that gave them little or no time
to pursue and develop new talent and, moreover, no American publisher had an adequate system of covering unso-
licited manuscripts or nursing along a promising talent.

The senior editors were consumed with manuscripts of
their published writers plus a never ending round of sales
conferences, making contracts, swimming the sea of cocktail
parties, giving lectures, attending the necessary Broadway
plays, and entertaining visiting firemen. Junior editors had
nearly no power to push a promising manuscript. Furthermore, the pressurized atmosphere of New York generally
lead to two or three martinis at lunch and watered down any
desire to delve into unpublished manuscripts from unknown
authors. David Shawcross commented that publishing was
the only business in the world that did nothing to perpetuate
itself. Every publisher had a history of allowing eventual
best sellers to slip through his hands, mainly through stu-
pidity.

Somewhere in every sludge pile there was a publishable
book or a potential author who needed a hand to "cross the
line." So he made an annual trip to America and dug. In a
decade Shawcross discovered a half dozen new American
authors including the sensational Negro James Morton Lin-
sey, who became a major literary figure.

Abraham Cady's manuscript sat on an agent's desk on a
day he was visited by David Shawcross. It had been taken
on by the agent on the recommendation of one of his authors,
who was a columnist on the *Virginia Pilot*, where Abe

worked as aviation editor. The book had been rejected seven times for seven different reasons.

That night at the Algonquin Hotel, Shawcross arranged a half dozen pillows around his back, adjusted the lamp, and laid out an array of tobacco. He perched his specs on his nose and balanced the blue-covered manuscript on his belly. As he turned the pages he dribbled ashes down his front, an absent-minded smoker of cigars, who left a telltale calling card of matches, ashes, burn holes, and an occasional flash fire in a wastebasket. At four o'clock in the morning he closed the manuscript of Abraham Cady's *The Brothers.* There were tears in his eyes.

Abe drew a deep breath as he entered the lobby of the Algonquin Hotel, that famed paneled domain of writers and actors. His voice was shaky as he asked for Mr. Shawcross's suite.

Abe knocked on the door of 408.

"Please come in." A plump, ruddy-cheeked tailored Englishman took his raincoat and hung it up. "Why you're no more than a boy," he said as he plopped into a high-backed chair with the manuscript spread on the coffee table before him. He thumbed through page after page, dripping a few ashes, brushing them off, then looked at the lad glued to the corner of the sofa and snatched off his glasses with a deliberate gesture.

"There's a million would be writers in this world to every writer," he said, "because they're thick-headed and too much in love with their own words to listen. Now, I think what you've got here shows promise but it needs work."

"I came to listen, Mr. Shawcross. I'll try not to be thick-headed but maybe I am, I don't know."

Shawcross smiled. Cady had his own mind, all right.

"I'll spend a few days working with you. The rest will be up to you."

"Thank you, sir. I got some time off from the paper in case it was needed."

"I am going to caution you, young Cady, that I've tried this many times and rarely succeeded. Most writers resent

criticism and those who don't mind and seem to understand
what I'm driving at lack the ability to comprehend and trans-
late it into publishable material. It's all very, very difficult."

"You'd better believe I'm going to make it," Abe said.

"Very well, I've booked a room for you down the hall.
Unpack your things and let's have a go at it."

For Abraham Cady, it was a luxurious experience. David
Shawcross showed why he was one of the world's best editors.
Not to write through Cady's pen but to get the best out of
Cady. Basic storytelling was the key most authors never
learn. Get the hero up a tree and cut the limb behind him.
Pace. Stopping a chapter at an exquisite instance of suspense.
Overwriting, the cardinal curse of all new authors. Under-
writing . . . throwing away in two lines a situation that
could be milked for several chapters. It is all right to lecture
as long as you lecture subtly but never let a speech interfere
with the flow of the story.

And the key trick that few novelists know. A novelist
must know what his last chapter is going to say and one way
or another work toward that last chapter. Too many writers
start with a good idea and carry it through the first chapters,
then fall apart because they had no idea where the top of
the mountain was in the first place.

At the end of three days, Abraham Cady had listened
carefully and questioned without anger. Abe returned to
Norfolk and began his rewrite. This, Shawcross told him,
the rewriting and rewriting separated the authors from the
would be authors.

When a young man sets sail on the sea of authorship he
is alone with little knowledge of the winds and tides and
swells and storms. There are so many questions that can only
be answered by persistence. And he went through it again,
the awful loneliness, the exhaustion, the rare instances of
exhilaration. And his book was done.

"Abe," Morris called over the phone. "There's a cablegram
for you."

"Read it, Poppa."

"O.K. It says, 'Manuscript received and read. Well done.

I will be pleased to publish it straight away. My regards and congratulations. Signed, David Shawcross.' "

The Brothers by Abraham Cady had an excellent reception in England. Old Shawcross had come up with another of his sleepers. It was a simple story, the author was not finely polished, but he struck at the heart. The novel said that because the Western Allies had betrayed Loyalist Spain there would be a great war. The price of diplomatic obscenity would be paid in the blood of millions of English, French, and Americans.

In America The Brothers was published by a firm who had originally rejected it (on the grounds it had nothing important to say) and it received an even greater acclaim, for it was published on the eve of World War II.

4

FROM THE TIME OF THE SELLOUT AT MUNICH POPPA TRIED EVERYTHING TO GET THE RELATIVES OUT OF POLAND BUT IT WAS IMPOSSIBLE. IN ADDITION TO HIS FATHER AND TWO BROTHERS THERE WERE SOME THIRTY OTHER COUSINS AND AUNTS AND UNCLES. AND THEN GERMANY ATTACKED POLAND. IT WAS A NIGHTMARE. FOR A SHORT TIME WE BREATHED EASIER, WHEN THE SOVIET UNION TOOK THE EASTERN PART OF POLAND WHICH HELD THE TOWN OF PRODNO. THEN THAT HOPE DIED WHEN GERMANY ATTACKED RUSSIA AND PRODNO FELL INTO GERMAN HANDS.

POPPA'S ATTITUDE ABOUT FASCISM CHANGED. BEN'S DEATH AND THE FEAR FOR HIS FAMILY TURNED HIM INTO A MILITANT. I KNEW IT WOULD BE TERRIBLE FOR THEM WHEN I DECIDED TO GO TO WAR, BUT I COULDN'T WAIT.

IN THE FALL OF 1941 I ENLISTED IN THE ROYAL CANA-
DIAN AIR FORCE IN ORDER TO GET TO ENGLAND AND JOIN
THE EAGLE SQUADRON OF AMERICAN VOLUNTEERS. LIKE
BEN'S LACALLE SQUADRON IT WAS A HELL BENT GANG,
BLAKESLEE, GENTILE, CHESLEY PETERSON, AND A LOT OF
OTHERS WHO MADE NAMES AS FIGHTER PILOTS. FUNNY
PART OF IT WAS THAT MANY OF THEM HAD WASHED OUT
OF THE AMERICAN ARMY AIR CORPS FOR INABILITY TO
FLY.

POPPA MADE A SMALL PROTEST ARGUING THAT AMER-
ICA WOULD SOON BE IN THE WAR SO WHY SHOULD I GO
OUT SPORTING FOR TROUBLE. MOMMA WAS WORSE. SHE
FEARED SHE WOULD END UP LOSING BOTH OF HER SONS.
THEY GAVE IN. POPPA CONFIDED THAT HE WAS PROUD
AND MOMMA SAID THINGS LIKE, "TRY TO BE CAREFUL
AND DON'T BE A HERO."

I WAS PRETTY SCARED WHEN I KISSED THEM GOOD-BY
AND BOARDED THE TRAIN FOR TORONTO. A FEW MONTHS
AFTER I STARTED TRAINING AS A SPITFIRE PILOT, AMER-
ICA WAS ATTACKED AT PEARL HARBOR.

August 19, 1942

Seven thousand Canadians and British Commandos poured
ashore at the French beach resort of Dieppe on a reconnais-
sance raid to test the German coastal defenses.

Engineers moving behind the infantry reached and spiked
some large German guns but the operation ran into serious
trouble quickly. One flank was hit by a German flotilla and
in the center, Canadian tanks were hung up on the sea wall
and then the German counterattack turned the raid into a
disaster.

Overhead, a blizzard of Spitfires and Messerschmitts raged
in a massive dogfight while other allied planes came in low
to cover the disaster on the beach. Among them were the
American Eagles and their youngest pilot, twenty-two-year-
old Abraham Cady flying his fifth mission.

As the planes ran low on fuel and ammunition they
streaked back to England to refuel and load and return to the
action. Abe came back to Dieppe on his third sortie of the

day as the airmen desperately attempted to stall the German counterattack.

Working at treetop level he made pass after pass at a German company crawling out of the woods. With communications largely broken and squadrons scattered all over the sky it became increasingly difficult to warn comrades in trouble. They were all on their own.

Abe swooped down on a bridge and sprayed it clean of the enemy, when a trio of Messerschmitts pounced on him from the cover of a cloud. He peeled off deftly to evade and just as he felt he had slipped away his plane shuttered violently under the impact of a striking of machine gun bullets. The controls jerked his arms half out of their sockets, and he started to spin. Abe muscled her back into control, but she veered crazily like a toy glider in a windstorm.

JESUS H. CHRIST ON A CRUTCH! MY TAIL'S SHOT UP. DITCH HER? HELL NO, NOT OVER WATER. SHAG ASS FOR ENGLAND. LORD, GIVE ME THIRTY MINUTES.

Abe jockeyed his swerving craft a few hundred feet over the Channel racing for England. Fifteen minutes to land, ten . . .

"Zenith, Zenith, this is Dog Two Dog on red alert. I'm shot up."

"Hello, Dog Two Dog. This is Zenith. What are your intentions?"

SONOFABITCH!

A Messerschmitt came up behind Abe. Using every ounce of his strength he pulled the nose of his plane up and into a deliberate stall. The startled German was unable to duplicate the maneuver and passed beneath him. Abe let her dive and pressed the triggers.

"I've got him! I've got him!"

HANG ON. THANK GOD . . . COAST OF ENGLAND. CHRIST, I CAN'T HOLD MY ALTITUDE. EASY BABY, EASY, YOU'RE RIPPING MY ARMS OUT.

He veered at the mainland at a sharp angle.

"Hello, Dog Two Dog. This is Drewerry. We see you now. We're advising you to ditch."

"I can't. I'm too low to jump. I'm going to have to land her."

"Cleared to land."

The sirens at Drewerry set off a scramble of activity. Fire wagons and an ambulance and a rescue squad inched up the apron next to the runway as the wounded bird augered in.

"Poor devil, he's really out of control."

"Hang on there, Yank."

BOY, I DO NOT LIKE THIS ANGLE. I DO NOT LIKE IT AT ALL. COME ON, SWEETHEART, LINE UP WITH THAT RUNWAY. THAT'S A GOOD GIRL. NOW JUST HOLD IT.

Three hundred, two hundred, cut engine, glide, glide. "Look at that lad fly!"

COME ON, GROUND, LET ME FEEL YOU. COME ON, GROUND. OH BOY, DOES THAT FEEL . . . JESUS! MY FUCKING LANDING GEAR IS BUSTED.

Abe pulled up his landing gear and set her down on her belly. The Spitfire careened off the runway with sparks flying. At the last instant he veered away from a barracks and tore for the woods, then mangled to a halt in the trees. The sirens screamed and bore down on him. Abe shoved the canopy back and crawled out on the wing. Then after a beat of silence a terrible explosion was followed by billowing flames!

5

OH MY GOD! I'M DEAD! I KNOW I'M DEAD! GOD! I CAN'T
SEE! I CAN'T MOVE! MY HEAD IS BLURRED!

"Help me!" Abe cried.

"Lieutenant Cady," a woman's voice penetrated the darkness, "can you hear me?"

"Help me," he cried, "where am I? What's happened to me?"

"Lieutenant Cady," the voice said again. "If you hear me, please say so."

"Yes," he gasped.

"I'm Sister Grace, a nurse, and you're in the RAF Hospital near Bath. You've been badly hurt."

"I'm blind. Oh God, I'm blind!"

"Will you try to get control of yourself so we can speak?"

"Touch me so I know you're here."

He forced himself to gain control.

"You've undergone a serious operation," Sister Grace said, "and you're all bandaged up. Don't be frightened because you can't see or move. Let me go and get the doctor, and he'll explain everything to you."

"Please don't go away for long."

"I'll be right back. You must remain calm now."

He sucked in air deeply and quivered in fear. His heart raced to urgent footsteps he could hear coming toward him.

"Woke up, have you," a commanding British voice said. "I'm Dr. Finchly."

"Tell me, Doctor, tell me if I'm blind."

"No," the doctor answered. "You've had quite a bit of sedation and your mind is apt to be rather fuzzy. Are you able to comprehend?"

"Yes, I'm a little cuckoo, but I understand."

"Very well, then," Finchly said, sitting on the edge of the bed. "You've lost the sight of your right eye, but we're going to be able to save the other one."

"Are you sure?"

"Yes, we're quite certain of it."

"What happened?"

"Let me explain it to you in simple terms. Your aircraft exploded shortly after you ran into the woods. You were crawling on the wing at the time and at the instant of explosion your hands went up over your face to protect it."

"I remember that much."

"The backs of your hands took most of the shock and were severely burned. Third degree burns. Now, you have four tendons on each hand like rubber bands to each finger. These may be damaged. If the burns don't heal properly we will have to do a skin graft and if the tendons have been damaged we'll do tendon grafts. Do you understand me so far?"

"Yes, sir."

"In any event we will be able to restore full use of both hands. It may take time, but we're very, very successful with both skin and tendon grafts."

"What about my eyes," he whispered.

"With the explosion, some minute fragments hit both your eyes perforating your cornea. The cornea is a thin membrane that covers the eye. Now, each eye is filled with a substance that appears somewhat like egg albumin that keeps it inflated like air in a tire. Your right eye was deeply penetrated, the fluid leaked and the entire eyeball collapsed."

"As for the other eye, everything was intact except for the perforation of the cornea. We had to replace it with a substitute cornea. The way we did this was to dissect the upper membrane of your eyelid and cover the eye with it, stitching it to the bottom of the lid. The stitches are thinner than a strand of human hair."

"When can I know if I can see?"

"Well, I promise you, you have vision in your left eye but there are two problems you're going to have to face up to. A fatty embolism can form from the damage to your hands and move up to your eye and destroy further tissue. Secondly, you are suffering from a rather severe concussion from the blast which would put normal vision out of focus.

We'll allow you to see for a few minutes each day, when we change bandages and treat your eye and hands."

"O.K.," Abe said, "I'll be good . . . and thanks, Doctor."

"Quite all right. Your publisher, Mr. Shawcross, has been waiting here for almost three days."

"Sure," Abe said.

"Well, Abe," Shawcross said, "they said you did some fancy flying to get back across the Channel and that was quite a trick getting your landing gear up and avoiding the barrack."

"Yeah, I'm a hell of a flyer."

"Is it all right if I smoke, Doctor."

"Certainly."

Abe liked the smell of Shawcross's cigar. It reminded him of those days in New York, when they worked day and night on his manuscript.

"My parents know about this?"

"I induced them not to inform your mother and father until you could send word, personally."

"Thanks. Jesus, I sure bought the farm."

"Bought a farm?" Dr. Finchly asked.

"It's an American phrase. It means he got a bashing about."

"Yes, rather, I'd say."

Dear Momma and Poppa:

You shouldn't be alarmed because this letter isn't in my handwriting. The reason I'm not personally writing for a while is that I got into a slight accident and burned my hands a little.

Let me assure you I'm otherwise in good health, in a fine hospital and there is no permanent damage of any kind. Even the food here is good.

I had a little trouble landing my plane and so forth. I probably won't be flying anymore because they're so sticky about perfect health.

There's a nice young lady here who takes my letters and she's happy to let me write to you every few days.

Mainly, you're absolutely not to worry for a minute.
Love to Sophie and everyone.

Your devoted son,

Abe

6

PATIENCE.

IF I EVER HEAR THAT WORD AGAIN, I'M GOING TO FLIP
MY LID. PATIENCE, THAT'S WHAT THEY TELL ME
TWENTY TIMES A DAY. PATIENCE.

I LIE FROZEN ON MY BACK IN TOTAL DARKNESS. WHEN
THE EFFECT OF THE DRUGS WEARS OFF THE PAINS IN
MY HANDS BECOME EXCRUCIATING. I PLAY GAMES. I
PLAY OUT A BASEBALL GAME PITCH BY PITCH. I'M THE
RED SOX PITCHER. IN ONE GAME I STRUCK OUT THE
WHOLE YANKEE LINE-UP. RIZZUTO, GORDON, DICKEY,
KELLER. DIMAGGIO WAS LAST. WE GOT TO THREE AND
TWO. HE'S DUG IN TO SAVE THE YANKEE REPUTATION. I
GIVE HIM LOT OF MOTION AND DISH UP A SLOW CURVE.
IT TAKES GUTS TO THROW THAT PITCH IN SUCH A SIT-
UATION. DIMAGGIO NEARLY BROKE HIS BACK DIVING
AFTER IT. NINE STRAIGHT YANKEES. IT'S A FEAT THAT
WILL STAND IN THE RECORD BOOKS FOR YEARS.

I THINK ABOUT THE WOMEN I'VE SLEPT WITH. I'M
STILL A KID SO A DOZEN ISN'T BAD. BUT I CAN'T REMEM-
BER MOST OF THEIR NAMES.

I THINK ABOUT BEN. GOD, I MISS BEN. WHAT A
WINNER I AM. I WANTED THREE THINGS IN MY LIFE;
TO PLAY BALL, TO FLY, AND TO WRITE. TWO OF THEM
ARE GONE FOREVER AND HOW CAN I WRITE, WITH MY
PECKER?

ANYHOW, THESE PEOPLE HERE ARE REALLY WONDER-

FUL. THEY TREAT ME LIKE A PORCELAIN DOLL. EVERY-
THING I DO BECOMES AN INVOLVED CHORE. IF SOMEONE
LEADS ME TO THE BATHROOM AND SETS ME ON THE
POT I CAN DO MY BUSINESS BUT THEN SOMEBODY'S
GOT TO WIPE ME. I CAN'T EVEN AIM TO TAKE A LEAK.
I'VE GOT TO SIT LIKE A WOMAN. IT'S ABSOLUTELY HUMIL-
IATING.

EVERYDAY THEY LET ME OUT OF MY MUMMY CAGE
FOR A FEW MINUTES. MY GOOD EYE IS USUALLY GLUED
SHUT. BY THE TIME I GET IT INTO FOCUS THEY'RE
WRAPPING ME UP AGAIN. I KEEP TELLING MYSELF IT
COULD BE WORSE. EVERYDAY THE EYE IS LESS BLURRED
AND I'M STARTING TO GET SOME MOVEMENT IN MY
HANDS.

DAVID SHAWCROSS COMES FROM LONDON ONCE OR
TWICE A WEEK. HIS WIFE, LORRAINE, NEVER FAILS TO
BRING A PACKAGE OF FOOD. SHE'S AS BAD AS MOMMA. I
KNOW IT'S COSTING HER VALUABLE RATION COUPONS,
AND I TRY TO TELL HER THEY'RE FEEDING ME LIKE
ROYALTY.

HOW I WELCOME THE SMELL OF THAT STINKY CIGAR.
SHAWCROSS HAS ALL BUT GIVEN UP PUBLISHING TO
WORK FOR THE GOVERNMENT TO NEGOTIATE A BOOK
EXCHANGE PROGRAM WITH THE RUSSIANS. HIS STORIES
OF THE PARANOID BEHAVIOR AT THE SOVIET EMBASSY
ARE A RIOT.

MY BUDDIES VISIT ONCE IN A WHILE BUT IT'S A LONG
TRIP FOR THEM. THE EAGLE SQUADRON HAS BEEN TRANS-
FERRED OUT OF THE RAF INTO THE AMERICAN AIR
CORPS. SO, I DON'T KNOW WHAT I AM. I'M NOT MUCH
USE TO ANYONE, ANYHOW.

A MONTH PASSES. PATIENCE, THEY TELL ME. JESUS,
I HATE THAT WORD. THEY'RE GOING TO START SKIN
GRAFTS SOON.

THEN SOMETHING HAPPENED AND THE DAYS DIDN'T
SEEM SO LONG OR AGONIZING AFTER THAT. HER NAME
IS SAMANTHA LINSTEAD, AND HER FATHER IS A SQUIRE
WITH AN OLD FAMILY FARM IN THE MINDIP HILLS NOT
FAR FROM BATH. SAMANTHA IS TWENTY AND A RED

CROSS VOLUNTEER AIDE. AT FIRST SHE CAME IN ON ROUTINE THINGS LIKE TAKING LETTERS AND SPONGING ME OFF. WE GOT TO TALKING A LOT AND PRETTY SOON SHE BROUGHT HER PHONOGRAPH AND SOME RECORDS AND A RADIO SET. SHE'D SPEND A GOOD PART OF THE DAY IN MY ROOM, FEEDING ME, HOLDING MY CIGARETTE, AND SHE READ A LOT TO ME.

CAN A MAN FALL IN LOVE WITH A VOICE?

I NEVER SAW HER. SHE ALWAYS CAME AFTER MY MORNING TREATMENT. ALL I KNEW WAS HER VOICE. I SPENT HALF MY TIME IMAGINING WHAT SHE LOOKED LIKE. SHE INSISTED SHE WAS VERY PLAIN.

ABOUT A WEEK AFTER SHE CAME I WAS ABLE TO TAKE SHORT WALKS WITH HER LEADING ME AROUND THE HOSPITAL GROUNDS. AND THEN, SHE GOT TO TOUCHING ME MORE AND MORE.

"Light me up, Sam," Abe said.

Samantha sat near the bed and held the cigarette carefully as he puffed. When she snuffed it out, she slipped her hand through the opening of his pajamas and rubbed the tips of her fingers over his chest, barely making contact.

"Sam, I've been thinking. Maybe you'd better not come back to see me, any more." Her hand drew away from him suddenly. "I don't like the idea of anyone feeling sorry for me."

"Do you think that's why I come here?"

"You lie in darkness all day and all night and your mind can play tricks. I'm starting to take things more serious than I ought to. You've been a real wonderful person and shouldn't be a victim of my fantasies."

"Abe. Don't you know how wonderful it is for me to be with you? Maybe when we see each other you won't care for me, but I don't want to change anything now. And you're not going to get rid of me that easily, and you really aren't in much of a condition to do anything about it."

Samantha's car passed on to the circular driveway of Linstead Hall. The tires crunched over the gravel and then halted before a small manor house of two centuries ago.

"There's Mommy and Daddy. This is Abe. You can't see too much of him, but his photographs are quite handsome."

"Welcome to Linstead Hall," Donald Linstead said.

"Pardon my gloves," Abe answered, holding up his bandaged hands.

She led him carefully through a wooded land and then found a soft place in a meadow looking down on the manor and she described the scene to him.

"I can smell cows and horses and smoke and all kinds of flowers. It must be beautiful up here. I can't tell one flower from the other."

"There's heather and roses and the fires are coming from the peat bogs."

Oh Abe! she thought. I do love you.

On the third visit to Linstead Hall the family received the happy news that Abe's eye bandages would be removed for a few hours each day.

Samantha seemed edgy during the walk. In the darkness, one can sense things fiercely. The tone of her voice was different, the vibrations were tense.

It had been a long day and Abe was tired. A male nurse came in from the village to bathe and change him. Afterward he stretched out on the bed, grumbling over his entombed hands. Patience. To be able to shave, to be able to blow my nose, to be able to read.

To be able to see Samantha.

He heard the door open and close and could tell by the turn of the knob it was Samantha.

"I hope I didn't awaken you."

"No."

The bed sank as she sat beside him. "It's going to be a great event when they take those bandages off your eyes. I mean your eye. You've been very brave."

"Like I had a choice. Well, we sure know what humility is."

Abe could hear the soft sobs she was trying to stifle. He wanted to reach out for her as he had wanted to a hundred times. What did she feel like. Were her breasts large or small. Was her hair soft. Were her lips sensuous.

"What the hell are you crying for?"

"I don't know." They both knew. In a sad strange way they had experienced something totally unique and it was going to come to an end and neither of them knew if the ending was final or would ignite a new beginning. Samantha was afraid she would be rejected.

She lay beside him as they had done after their walks, and her fingers unbuttoned his shirt, and she laid her cheek on his chest and then her hands and lips became like whispers all about his body.

"I talked to the doctor," she said. "He told me it would be all right," and she reached between his legs. "Just be still, I'll do everything."

She undressed him and flung her own clothing off and locked the door.

Oh, fantastic darkness! Every sensation was so vivid, the gentle slaps, the kissing of his feet, the feather soft whip of her hair. Samantha was in a controlled frenzy as he succumbed to her.

And then she cried and told him she had never been so happy, and Abe said he was really a better lover but under the circumstances he was glad some part of him worked. And then the love talk became silly, and they laughed because it was really quite funny.

7

David Shawcross's phone rang angrily. He groped for the bed lamp, yawned his way to a sitting position. "Good God," he mumbled, "it's three in the morning."

"Hello!"

"Mr. Shawcross?"

"Yes, this is Shawcross."

"Sergeant Richardson, Military Police attached to the station in Marylebone Lane, sir."

"Richardson, it's three o'clock in the morning. Get on with it, man."

"So sorry to disturb you, sir. We've picked up an officer, RAF chap, a Lieutenant Abraham . . . C . . . A . . . D . . . Y, Cady."

"Abe in London?"

"Yes, sir. He was rather intoxicated when we picked him up. Drunk as a lord if you don't mind me saying, sir."

"Is he all right, Richardson?"

"In a manner of speaking, sir. There was a note pinned to his uniform. Shall I read it?"

"Yes, by all means."

" 'My name is Abraham Cady. If I appear to be drunk, don't be confused. I am having a case of bends due to tunnel work on a secret project and must be decompressed slowly. Deposit my body to David Shawcross, 77 Cumberland Terrace. NW 8.' Will you accept him, Mr. Shawcross? Don't want to press charges on the chap, just out of the hospital and all that."

"Charges. For what?"

"Well, sir, when we got to him he was swimming in the fountain in Trafalgar Square . . . nude."

"Bring the bugger over, I'll take him."

"So you were a German U-boat, were you now?" Shawcross taunted.

Abe groaned through one more cup of black coffee. At least the British call it coffee. Ugh!

"Flaunting your up-periscope in the middle of our stately fountain. Really, Abraham."

"Shawcross, put out the goddam cigar. Can't you see I'm dying."

"More coffee, dear?" Lorraine asked.

"God no. I mean, no thanks."

She tinkled a bell for the maid and helped her clear the

dishes. "I've got to be trotting off. The queues are still dreadful and I've got to stock up. Our kiddies are coming down from Manchester tomorrow." She kissed Abe's cheek. "I do hope you're feeling better, dear."

When she left, David grumbled. "I suppose I love my grandchildren as much as the next grandfather but frankly, they're spoiled little bastards. I keep writing Pam and telling her how dangerous it is here in London but damned if she'll listen. Anyhow, I've been thinking seriously about taking Geoff into the business after the war. Now what's all this nonsense about you and this girl, Pinhead, Greenbed . . ."

"Linstead. Samantha Linstead."

"Are you in love with her or what?"

"I don't know. I've never seen her. I've made love to her, but I've never seen her or touched her."

"Nothing really strange about that. All lovers are blind in one way or another. I've seen her. She's rather attractive, in an outdoorsy sort of way. Sturdy type."

"She stopped coming to the hospital when they took the bandages off my eyes. She was afraid I wouldn't like her. I was never so damned miserable in my life. I wanted to go beat the manor house door down and claim her, then I got all choked up, too. Suppose she was a real dog? Suppose she got a good look at me in the daylight and got sober? Stupid, isn't it?"

"Very. Well, you'll have to take a look at each other sooner or later. In the meanwhile do you have any company to forget Samantha with?"

"No, I'm out of touch in London," Abe said. "The first four calls I made last night, two were married, one pregnant, and on the fourth call a man answered."

"Well, let's see," Shawcross said, diving his pudgy fingers into his vest and fishing out an address book. As he thumbed it he grunted in delight a few times. "Why don't you meet me for lunch at Mirabelle's at two. We ought to be able to come up with something."

Abraham Cady, sobered and reassembled, turned Curzon Street all filled with the electricity of wartime London and

into the plush sanctuary of Mirabelle's. The maître d' was
expecting him. Abe stood a moment and looked over the
room to Shawcross's traditional table. He had come up with
a redhead. Very British looking. Nice body from what he
could see. Didn't look too stupid. Seemed nervous. That was
par. Everyone gets nervous before meeting a writer and
usually disappointed afterward. They expect nothing but
gems to flow from the writer's brilliant mind.

"Ah, Abraham," Shawcross said, struggling out of his seat.
Meet Cynthia Greene. Cynthia is a secretary to one of my
colleagues in the publishing business and is an admirer of
your book."

Abe took the girl's hand warmly as he always took a
woman's hand. It was a bit damp with nerves but otherwise
firm. A handshake told so much. He detested the wet limp
fish so many women gave. She smiled. The game was on. He
sat down.

Nice going, Shawcross, Abe thought.

"Waiter, a little nip of the hair that killed the dog for my
friend here."

"Whisky, over ice," Abe ordered.

Shawcross commented that ice was barbaric and Abe told
about an English girl he knew who drank a pint and a half
of Scotch each and every day but would never take ice because she was afraid it would wreck her liver.

Cheers. They sipped and studied the fragile wartime
menu. Abe surveyed Miss Greene.

The first thing he liked aside from her general looks and
firm handshake was that she was obviously an English lady
and kept her mouth shut. All women have volcanoes. Some
compulsively erupted from the mouth with unending dribble.
Other women kept their volcanoes dormant and exploded
them at the right time in the right way. Abe liked quiet
women.

The captain handed David Shawcross a note. He adjusted
his specs and grumbled. "I know this sounds like an obvious
ploy to get you two alone but the Russians have called me.
Uncivilized bastards. Try to muddle through without me.

Now, don't you try to steal my writer for your house. He's due for a good book, soon."

They were alone.

"How long have you known Shawcross?" Abe asked.

"Since he began visiting you in the hospital."

There was no mistaking that voice. "Samantha?"

"Yes, Abe."

"Samantha."

"Mr. Shawcross loves you like a son. He phoned me this morning and told me you cried half the night. I'm sorry I ran. Well, here I am. I know you're terribly disappointed."

"No . . . no . . . you're just lovely."

8

From a meadow in the Mindip Hills Abe and Samantha watched wave after wave of airplanes flying toward the Continent. The sky was black with them. Lumbering bombers and swarms of fighters. They passed and their sounds faded and the sky was blue. Abe stared pensively down to Linstead Hall.

Samantha felt a sudden chill. She placed her sweater on her shoulders. The flowers bent to the breeze and her soft red hair danced. She went so well with the countryside. Samantha looked as though she were born riding a horse.

The hospital agreed that he could take a furlough as long as he reported for twice weekly treatments. Dr. Finchly also strongly advised Abe to stay out of London. He needed the peace of Linstead Hall. Heather and horse manure. But the daily flights of planes constantly reminded him that there was a war out there.

"So pensive," Samantha said.

"The war is passing me by," he said.

"I know you're restless but when all is said and done

perhaps you were never meant to be anything but a writer. I know you've a book churning inside you."

"My hands. They start to hurt after just a few minutes. I may have to have one more operation, yet."

"Abe, have you ever thought of me being your hands?"

"I don't know if you can write a book that way . . . I just don't know."

"Why don't we try."

The thought of it brought Abraham Cady to life. It was very awkward at first and difficult to share a novelist's thoughts. Each day he became better able to organize his mind. He learned to dictate until he was capable of pouring out a torrent of words.

The furlough ended. Abe was discharged from the Air Corps. A farewell bust at the Officer's Club with his old buddies and back to Linstead Hall to write.

Samantha became the silent partner and privileged observer to one of the most unique of all human experiences, the writing of a novel. She saw him detach himself from the first world of reality and submerge into the second world of his own creation and wander through it alone. There was no magic. There was no inspiration that people always look for and imagine in the writer. What there was was a relentless plodding requiring a special kind of stamina that makes the profession so limited. Of course there came those moments when things suddenly fell into a natural rhythm and even more rare, that instant of pure flying through creative exhilaration.

But what Samantha witnessed most was the uncertainty, the drain, the emotional downs, the exhaustion. Those times he did not have the strength to eat or undress himself.

David Shawcross stood in the wings, a happy man knowing exactly when to make Abe turn it off with a blast in London. A roaring drunk. A flushing out, and a return to the blank sheet of paper. He told Samantha that Abe had within him the key to greatness on one major premise. He was aware of his weaknesses as a writer as well as his strengths; Shawcross said few writers had the ability of introspection because they were too vain to admit weakness. This was

Abraham Cady's power, and he controlled his second novel. He was in his twenties and writing like sixty.

The Jug (a nickname for the P-47 Thunderbolt) was a simple and classical story of men at war. The hero was Major General Vincent Bertelli, a second generation street fighter of Italian-American descent. An officer in the early thirties he rose quickly in the war that had become air oriented. Bertelli was a relentless and apparently heartless driver who was ready to take heavy losses in dangerous raids on the thesis that "war was war."

The general's son, Sal, flew as a squadron commander in his father's command. The deep love between them is camouflaged by what appears to be father/son hatred.

General Bertelli orders a raid and places his son's squadron in a suicide position. The news of Sal's death is delivered by Barney, the sole survivor in the squadron.

Bertelli listens without emotion and is spat upon by Barney.

"You're tired," the general said, "I'll forget about this."

Barney turned on his heel. "Barney!" the general commanded and he halted. Bertelli wanted desperately to show his son's transfer order and to tell him he pleaded with Sal to quit. His boy had refused despite everyone knowing he had flown himself into exhaustion.

"Never mind," General Bertelli said.

And suddenly Barney knew. "I'm sorry, sir. He just had to go on proving himself, like he had no choice."

"It's a fucking war," the general answered, "people are going to get hurt. Get some rest, Barney. You're going up again in a few hours. Big target. U-boat pens."

The door closed. General Bertelli opened the top drawer of his desk and swallowed a nitroglycerin tablet for the attack that was coming on. "Sal," he said, "I loved you. Why couldn't I tell you."

"The end," Abe's hoarse voice rasped. He stood behind Samantha and watched her type those two beautiful last words.

"Oh, Abe," she cried, "it's lovely."

"I need a belt," he said.

When she left he took her place at the typewriter and pecked out with stiff fingers, "Dedicated to Samantha with love," and then the words . . . "will you marry me?"

9

Little by little full use of Abe's hands returned. An eye patch covered his deformity. Abraham Cady was a one-eyed, broken winged eagle, but an eagle, nonetheless. After his discharge and with his book, *The Jug*, selling well, he signed on with United Press in London.

London was a vital place, the heartbeat of the free world building up to burst upon the European Continent aware fully of its own importance and rife with the colors of Allied and Empire troops and those of governments in exile. The smoke of German incendiaries had long died out in the gutted center of London. The nights in the tubes were over but there were still queues, the eternal British queues and sandbags and balloon barrages and blackouts and then the buzz bombs.

Abraham Cady joined a fraternity of those men charged with the mission of telling the story and in these days in London it was a legendary roll call from Quentin Reynolds to Edward R. Murrow on their news beats from the American Embassy to Downing Street to BBC House to the great press artery of Fleet Street.

The Linsteads had traditionally kept a small town house in London in Colchester Mews off Chelsea Square. The mews were once carriage houses and servants quarters behind the stately five story homes bordering London's green squares. After the First World War, when horses faded from the scene, the mews were converted into doll house quarters that were particularly attractive to writers, musicians, actors, and visiting squires.

Abe and Samantha moved into the mews after their wedding at Linstead Hall, and he went searching for a part of the war.

At a time and place that distinguished journalism was commonplace Abe Cady was able to carve a distinctive niche as the flyer's correspondent.

From those first floundering days of the Battle of Britain, all of England became a massive airfield. The British owned the night and the American Eighth Air Force mastered the European skies by day with raids deep into Germany now escorted by swarms of Mustang fighters.

Abe flew with the Halifaxes by night and Flying Fortresses by day, and he wrote of a sort of fairyland war of seemingly harmless puffs of smoke down "flak alley" and the great swirling ballets of the dogfights. He wrote of the blissful numbness of total exhaustion to the lullaby of five thousand droning engines. And blood. A tail or belly gunner cut in half and men struggling to free him from his prison. Of long streams of smoke and crippled birds struggling in a place out of their element to find the earth again. And sentimental songs around the bars, of silent stares at the empty bunks. Of varnished officers poring over blown-up maps of Germany with a crisp detached vernacular. And the view from the sky as their loads of death rained down on miniature sets that were the cities of Germany.

WE'LL BE OVER BERLIN IN A HALF HOUR. THE ARMADA OUTSIDE HAS BLACKENED THE SKY LIKE A SWARM OF LOCUSTS. WE ARE CLOAKED WITH FIGHTER PLANES OF THE WOLF PACK FLYING RAMROD TO ESCORT THE BOMBERS.

A STARTLED COMMUNICATION. "LOOK OUT, TONY, MESSERS AT SEVEN O'CLOCK."

A SHORT, WILD DOGFIGHT BELOW US. A SCARLET-NOSED MUSTANG BELCHES SMOKE AND SPIRALS EARTHWARD WITH A MESSERSCHMITT ON HIS TAIL. OUR KID MUST HAVE BEEN GREEN. THE MESSERS ARE NO MATCH FOR THE MUSTANG. THE KRAUT HAD TO BE GOOD TO HAVE SURVIVED THIS LONG. THE MUSTANG ERUPTS. IT'S DONE. NO PARACHUTE.

LATER I LEARNED HE WAS A SECOND YEAR ENGINEER-
ING STUDENT AT GEORGIA TECH. WHAT WILL IT BE LIKE
TOMORROW IN ATLANTA WHEN THE CABLEGRAM AR-
RIVES AND THE LIVES OF A DOZEN PEOPLE FALL TO A
GRIEF-STRICKEN WHISPER. HE WAS THE ONLY MALE
HEIR. THE ONE WHO WAS GOING TO CARRY THEIR NAME
INTO THE NEXT GENERATION.

THE KRAUTS HAVE BEEN BEATEN OFF. IT COST FOUR
MUSTANGS AND TWO BOMBERS. BOMBERS DIE SLOWER.
WRITHE IN AGONY, TWIST AND ROLL HEAVILY. DESPER-
ATE MEN TUG AT CANOPIES. AND THEN, DISINTEGRATION.

TENSING UP AND ALERT AS WE NEAR BERLIN. ALL EX-
CEPT THE CO-PILOT ASLEEP TWISTED LIKE A PRETZEL
THAT ONLY A YOUNG MAN COULD MANAGE. I'M INVITED
TO TAKE THE CONTROLS.

MY HANDS ITCH WITH JOY AS I TAKE THE CONTROLS.
THE BOMBS FLOAT DOWN SLOWLY, DESCENDING LIKE A
MANTLE OF BLACK SNOW AND THEN GREAT GUSTS OF
ORANGE BILLOW FROM THE TORTURED CITY.

I AM SICK AT MY OWN ECSTASY AS OUR BATTERED
FLEET LIMPS BACK. WHY DOES MAN PUT HIS GREATEST
ENERGY AND TALENT INTO DESTRUCTION?

I AM THE WRITER. I MAKE IT ALL A MORALITY PLAY.
WE'RE WHITE UP HERE, LIKE ANGELS. THEY'RE BLACK
DOWN THERE LIKE DEVILS. DEVILS, ROAST IN HELL!

AND THEN I WONDER WHO I KILLED TODAY. AN EN-
GINEER LIKE THE BOY FROM GEORGIA, A MUSICIAN, A
DOCTOR, OR A CHILD WHO NEVER EVEN HAD A CHANCE
TO ASPIRE. WHAT A WASTE.

Samantha set the receiver down and grunted down-
heartedly. Her pregnancy had made her ill. She had been
queasy all day. She made her way up the narrow stairs to
the tiny bedroom where Abe lay in sprawled exhaustion.
For a moment she considered ignoring the phone call, but
he would be very angry. She tapped his shoulder.

"Abe."

"Uhhhh."

"We just got a call from Wing Commander Parsons at

Breedsford. They want you there by fourteen hundred."

I smell it, Abe thought. Ten to one they're going for the ball bearing works outside Hamburg. It will be one hell of a show. The night raids were more vivid in their sharp black and white contrasts. And after their pass, the carpet of red fires on the burning from the target. Abe popped off the bed and read his watch. Time for a shave and a bath.

Samantha appeared piqued and drawn. Her whiteness was even more apparent in London. "You mustn't be late," she said, "I'll draw your bath."

"You'll be all right, won't you, honey. I mean, about taking you out tonight. This raid must be a big one or Parsons wouldn't call."

"As a matter of fact, I'm not all right. Decent of you to ask, though."

"O.K., let's have it," Abe snapped.

"I'd rather you wouldn't speak to me as if I were on the carpet before the colonel's desk."

Abe grunted and tied on his robe. "What's wrong, honey?"

"I've been sick every morning for two weeks, but that's to be expected, I suppose. To escape the confinement of these four walls I get to stand in queues for hours on end or dive into the tube for my life ahead of the buzz bombs. And after living on scraps I'm jolly well homesick for Linstead Hall. I suppose it would be bearable if I saw anything of my husband. You crawl in, write your story and fall flat until the phone rings for the next raid. And those rare evenings you are in London you seem obsessed with shooting the breeze all night with David Shawcross or in some Fleet Street Pub."

"Finished?"

"Not really. I'm bloody bored and unhappy, but I don't think it means very much to you."

"Now, just hold on, Samantha. I happen to think we're goddam lucky. With fifty million men and women separated by this war we're plenty lucky to have a few hours together."

"Perhaps we would be if you weren't on a crusade to make every bombing mission out of England."

"That's my job."

"Oh, they all say you love your job. They say you're the best bomber jockey in both air forces."

"Come off it. They let me take the controls once in a while as a gesture."

"Not according to Commander Parsons. It's got to be a sign of luck if the old one-eyed eagle leads them in. Steady Abraham, he was known far and wide."

"My God, Samantha! What in the hell is so hard for you to understand. I hate fascism. I hate Hitler. I hate what the Germans have done to the Jewish people."

"Abe, you're shouting!" Samantha stiffened, breaking off the assault and quivering and sobbing to blunt male logic. "It's the loneliness," she cried.

"Honey, I . . . I don't know what to say. Loneliness is the brother of war and the mother of all writers. He asks his wife to endure it graciously because she will come to know that her ability to endure it can be her greatest gift."

"I don't understand you, Abe."

"I know."

"Well, don't act as if I'm some kind of clod. We have gone through a book together, you know."

"I didn't have hands so you owned me. Your possession of me was complete. When I had no sight and we made love you were your happiest because your possession was complete then, too. But now I've got my hands and eyes and you don't want to share me or understand what your end of this bargain consists of. It's going to be like this till the end of our lives, Samantha. It will always demand sacrifice and loneliness of both of us."

"You're great at twisting things to make me look very little."

"We're just starting out together, honey. Don't make the mistake of standing between me and my writing."

Samantha returned to Linstead Hall. After all, she was pregnant and life in London wasn't easy. Abe assured her he understood and then he went on with his war.

On D-Day, Ben Cady was born at Linstead Hall. His father, Abraham, wrote at the navigator's desk of a B-24

Liberator sent up from Italy for a saturation raid in conjunction with the invasion.

10

There are no J. Milton Mandelbaums, Abe thought. He's only a fiction from a bad Hollywood novel. He's only trying to act like a J. Milton Mandelbaum.

Mandelbaum, the young producing "genius" of American Global Studios, arrived in London to stir the hearts of man and produce the greatest aviation film of all times based on Abraham Cady's novel, *The Jug.*

He pitched tent in a three bedroom suite at the Savoy; the Oliver Messel Suite wasn't available at the Dorchester because of all the goddam brass and royalty in exile and that crap.

It was stocked to the gunnels with booze and broads and the kinds of things Englishmen had not seen in five years of war.

A 4-F in the draft (ulcers, eye astigmatism, psychosomatic asthma) he conned himself a "technical war correspondent's" rating and had a Saville Row tailor do him up a half dozen officer's uniforms.

"After all, Abe," he explained, "we're all in this thing together."

Abe suggested that if that was the case it would be good for Milton to fly a few bombing missions for first hand insight.

"Somebody's got to hold the old fort down here and get the old production rolling," Milton explained in passing on Abe's kind offer.

Milton always mentioned his own film first, the one which won an Oscar, somehow overlooking the fact it was based on a Hemingway story with the best director and screen writer in Hollywood working on it, and during most of the production he was in the hospital with an ulcer. An assistant (who was fired shortly after the film for disloyalty) had truly done the producing.

There were lengthy dissertations by him on his creative ability, his sincerity, his importance, the women (among them most of the NAME actresses) he had banged, his immaculate taste in all matters, his astute story instinct (if the studio would only get off my back I'd go back to writing. You and me are writers, Abe, we know the importance of the story), his house in Beverly Hills (pool, broads, limo, broads, sports cars, broads, servant, broads), the number of suits he owned, the extravagant gifts (he charged to the studio), his piousness (when I put up a window in the synagogue for my beloved father, I gave the temple an extra five thou), the people he knew by first name, the people who knew him by first name, the way the studio leaned on him for milestone decisions and his high ethical standards and his prowess at gin rummy and, of course, his modesty.

"Abe, we'll make them laugh, cry, die with those boys up there. I got a call into the front office. I'm pitching for Cary [Grant], Clark [Gable], or Spence [er Tracy] for the lead."

"But, Milt. Maybe Tracy but Grant and Gable aren't my idea of Italian fathers."

"Cary and Clark don't play anyone's father. You got to know actors, kid. They don't like growing old. Actually I had in mind using Cary for the part of Barney."

"Cary Grant, a twenty-three-year-old Jewish boy from the slums of New York?"

"We got to update a little. I was thinking of this General Bertelli character. Reads nice in the book, but do we really want to glorify wops when we're at war with them?"

"Bertelli is American born. . . ."

"Sure, I know that, you know that. But he's still a wop to the great American Midwest. If we make the Bertellis heroes the boys in the front office in New York will have a hemorrhage. After all they're banking and distributing the flick. There's rules. Don't glorify wops, nigs got to be dumb like animals, krauts have got to be comic, and most of all, don't say you're Jewish on the screen."